D1326914

THE PATIENT AT PEACOCKS HALL

THE PATIENT AT PEACOCKS HALL

Margery Allingham

Chivers Press • G.K. Hall & Co.
Bath, England • Thorndike, Maine USA

This Large Print edition is published by Chivers Press, England, and by G.K. Hall & Co., USA.

Published in 2000 in the U.K. by arrangement with Sexton Agency & Press Ltd.

Published in 2000 in the U.S. by arrangement with John Steven Robling, Ltd.

U.K. Hardcover   ISBN 0-7540-4121-2   (Chivers Large Print)
U.K. Softcover   ISBN 0-7540-4122-0   (Camden Large Print)
U.S. Softcover   ISBN 0-7838-8966-6   (Nightingale Series Edition)

The text of this Large Print edition is unabridged.
Other aspects of the book may vary from the original edition.

Set in 16 pt. New Times Roman.

Printed in Great Britain on acid-free paper.

British Library Cataloguing in Publication Data available

Library of Congress Cataloging-in-Publication Data

Allingham, Margery, 1904–1966.
    The patient at Peacocks Hall / Margery Allingham.
        p.   cm.
    ISBN 0-7838-8966-6 (lg. print : sc : alk. paper)
    1. Women physicians—Fiction. 2. Large type books.
    I. Title.
    PR6001.L678 P37   2000
    823'.912—dc21   00–021445

PART ONE

'I never did think her *eyes* were a patch on yours, Miss Ann. Take a good look. You can see them. They're as plain as anything. Now let me get you a hand mirror.'

Rhoda planted the folded newspaper with the photograph in it squarely in front of me, supporting it against my after-lunch coffee cup. She was forthright and innocently excited in every one of her two hundred pounds, and she tore open an old wound as surely as if, with her plump well-meaning fingers, she had found the cicatrix and ripped it from my flesh.

It was so unexpected. I had had such a busy morning and was so full of other people's troubles that my own life was utterly forgotten. She took me completely off guard and got right through at a stroke, without my being aware.

'No, thank you,' I said politely, hoping I had not turned white from the sudden frightening pain, for I know her so well that my armour slips into place by reflex action, and I knew she would be watching me anxiously to see if my recovery was complete. (Rhoda is the kind of woman who digs up the mint outside her kitchen door two days after she has planted it, to find out if it has started to grow.) 'I've seen my eyes this morning, bloodshot again. What do you think it is? Alcohol?'

She was nearly sidetracked. The buttons on

3

her white overall strained as she took a breath and peered at me.

'Nonsense, they're lovely, just like your poor mother's only a different blue and not so round.'

'How true,' I agreed. 'Like her, I've got two of them.'

'Now you're trying to be funny like your father. I never laughed when he wanted me to and I shan't at you. You have got nice eyes and you're getting quite good-looking altogether now you've finished working yourself to death at the hospital and settled down as half a country doctor. You've lost that puggy look you had. I was mentioning it to Mr. Dawson when he came with the veg.'

'That was interesting for him,' I murmured, remembering that gaunt, asthmatic greengrocer. 'I'm not half a doctor, by the way. I've been qualified for some years.'

'Four and a half,' she said. 'But you're an assistant to Dr. Ludlow, poor old gentleman, aren't you? You don't do it all yourself.' Her kind unlovely face wore its most characteristic expression, part suspicion, part belligerence and nearly all affection. 'Aren't you going to read the bit about *her*? Or perhaps you don't want to?'

I ignored the emphasis. Rhoda did not mean it, or at least not much. She was sixteen when she came to work for my mother three weeks after I was born, and now that there is only myself of the family left and I have my own little cottage at the far end of Dr. Ludlow's estate she has continued to work for me. She does it just as faithfully and a good deal more chattily than ever she did in that busy doctor's home in Southersham.

My father, who delighted in her and called her 'Rhododendron,' used to say that she was the only woman in the world who knew everything about him and understood absolutely nothing, but I think he did her less than justice. She understands, a little, not quite enough.

It was very pleasant in my room—or it had been before she brought the newspaper. The cottage has only one downstairs room other than the kitchen and it is a big one. It is furnished with the nicest bits from home and is long and low, with french windows giving onto a small mossy yard, and it looks onto the broad tree-islanded meadow which marks the end of the built-up area on this side of the little town of Mapleford.

I love it, and I was happy and peaceful and content before she spoke. Now, since she was watching me, I had to read the paragraph about Francia Forde.

I did not linger over the photograph. Let me be honest and say at once that I have never really studied any of the reproductions of that lovely Botticelli face with its halo of pale hair. I never saw any of the four films she starred in and I never let myself envisage her as a real woman, lest I should fall into that most self-punishing sin of all and hate her till I burned myself to ash. I had no idea if she was tall or short, shrill or husky, witty or a fool. As far as I was concerned, Francia Forde had never existed, nor John Linnett either.

Anyhow, that was my story and I was sticking to it, pretty well. I had my own way to make and I was enjoying it. At twenty-eight I was the chief assistant to an old man who had a practice twice too big for him. My experience was growing every hour. I liked my patients and their troubles were mine. I could still rejoice when they were born and feel a genuine pang when, despite my best efforts, they died. Love was now just another natural malady suffered or enjoyed by other people. I had experienced it, I knew about it, it was over.

At the moment my real passion was whooping cough. The paragraph could hardly, therefore, be expected to hold much interest for me, and I was surprised to find how difficult it was to read. I have no intention of reproducing it. I couldn't if I tried. The words danced before me and their sense didn't seem worth discovering. But it was something about the 'beautiful Francia Forde whom everyone had loved so much in *Shadow Lady*' having taken leave of the studios for a while to become the 'Moonlight Girl' in an enormous press advertising campaign which Moonlight Soap and Beauty Products Ltd. were about to launch on a breathless world—and there was a mention of television.

To me it simply meant that I was going to be reminded of her in every magazine or newspaper I opened, and that even the air would not be free of her. Movies I could and did avoid, but now she was going to be everywhere.

Rhoda had stamped off with the plates so I did not have to watch my face. I put the folded paper down and sat looking across the table at the rock flowers and the meadows beyond.

The past is a terrifying thing. One finds one cheats so. John was four years older than I. We were the children of friends. Our fathers were doctors in the same town and from our babyhood they had set their hearts first on our taking up medicine and then on our marrying. At that moment I could have sworn that it had all been a silly mistake of the old people's and that we never could have loved each other, and yet in the next instant I was remembering the night I first noticed John had grown so breathtakingly good-looking. It was the night before he was off to war as a fully fledged major in the R.A.M.C. and I was still in my first year at hospital. We had walked in the Linnetts' walled garden and the ilex trees had whispered above us and the sweet earth had breathed on us with a new tenderness.

7

Without wanting to in the least, as I sat there with Francia Forde's smile flashing up at me from the page, I remembered the feel of his fingers on my shoulder and the hard, unexpectedly importunate touch of his mouth on mine. I could understand still and even recapture all the crazy magic of that moment when we realised that the one really important thing in all the world was that we were ourselves and no one else, and that together we were complete and invincible.

All that was quite vivid. I could remember the plans we made and how none of them seemed at all grandiose or impossible. Even the children's clinic, which was to grow into a hospital and a research station, was more real to me than—say—the puzzled misery of the last time he came home on leave just after VE-Day.

By that time terrible things had happened. Old Dr. and Mrs. Linnett were both gone. They had stepped into a crowded train after a flying visit to London, only to be taken out in the screaming darkness in the midst of a raid two stations down the line. They were both dead, killed by machine-gun bullets, the surprised expression still on their kind old faces. My own father, too, was fuming in a bed in his own hospital as the cruelty of his last illness slowly consumed him.

I don't think John and I quarrelled on that last leave. We knew each other too well. We were still friends, still in love. We made plans for our wedding, which was to take place as soon as I had finished at St. James's. But there was a change in him. He had become nervy and preoccupied, as if the strain of war had begun to tell. At least, I think I put it down to the war. Women were just beginning to suspect that the experience might have had some sort of strange effect upon their menfolk about that time.

I know his looks had become remarkable. He had always been considered handsome in Southersham, but now there was something outstanding about him. He had his father's dark red hair and wide-shouldered height, his good head and wide smile, and he had Mrs. Linnett's short straight nose, thick creamy skin, and the narrow dancing eyes that were more attractive in a man even than in her. There was no doubt about it. Old friends, let alone strangers, looked hard at him twice and, if they happened to be young and female, were inclined to blush for no good reason at all. To do him justice—and it was terribly hard for me to do him justice at that distance—he had not seemed to be aware of any change.

I could remember all that, but later, that long lonely period in the winter of '45 when I had no letters, the time which seemed to go on for years—as I sat thinking that afternoon it had no reality for me. I had forgotten it. The psycho people have a theory that one only

9

remembers the things one desires to, secretly. I cannot believe that, for every line of the Southersham *Observer*'s bombshell that spring was as clear to me as if I had had the fuzzy small-town print before me, and if there was ever anything I should want to forget it must have been that. The owner and editor of that paper was my father's only local enemy. Daddy always said he had a 'corseted soul,' and certainly the way he presented that extract from the film company's publicity sheet was typical of him. He conveyed he did not approve of it but he got every word of it in.

Miss Phillimore sent the paper to me in London and I got it on a day that was pure poetry, green and gold, and blue skies. No one but she could have written, 'This may surprise you, dear,' in that spidery 1890 hand. The editor had quoted a few paragraphs written in the out-of-this-world style some of those writers achieve. I could recite them still, though I had only read them once.

FAIRYLIKE FRANCIA FORDE CAPTURES GLAMOUR HERO FROM ARMY.

Medicine Relinquishes Its Handsomest Man. Runaway Wedding Ere Film Goes on Floor. Francia Forde, Bullion's new and scintillating starlet, who is to portray the daughter (Yetta) in the new Dolores Duse

10

epic *Chains*, has married John Linnett, Director Waldo's latest discovery. Linnett, who has been granted indefinite leave from the army to play opposite his bride, will take the part of Yetta's tempestuous lover.

And so on and so on. There was a final line or so written in the same vein:

The Rumour Bird whispers to us that there is a certain little lady doctor in Linnett's home town who is going to feel badly over this development, but cheer up, Miss Medico, you can't keep a star on the ground—not when it's hitched to Francia's wagon.

The Southersham *Observer* finished the piece with a reference to 'an engagement notice printed in these columns not long ago,' and a snappy hark-back to the tragedy of Dr. and Mrs. Linnett's death in the raid.

I remembered that all right. Although I was heart-free and cured and wedded to whooping cough, I remembered every paralysing word of it. Incredibly enough, that was all there was to remember. That was all I ever heard. I had no letter, no message, not even gossip through friends. It was as though John had died. He had turned his back on his home, his ideals, and everything he had ever lived for. It was so unlike him that for months I could not believe it.

11

When *Chains* appeared, Francia was in it but not John. She made her first hit in that film in which Dolores Duse, the veteran French actress, was so moving, and in her, next film she was a star. Since then she had gone from strength to strength. But John had vanished. If he was still married to her, he kept in the background. He never wrote and he never came back to Southersham.

Well, there it was, that was my story, and if I have not forgotten quite as completely as I had thought, I had at least got over it. That afternoon I honestly believe that the only thing I still felt I could not forgive John for was the waste, the wicked betrayal of his career. That was something a million times more important than I could ever be, and yet . . .

Old Dr. Percy Ludlow saved me from myself just then. I glanced up to see him trotting across the meadow and I got up to open the glass doors to meet him. Anyone less like the popular conception of a doctor I have yet to see. He is a tough, slightly horsy little man with a face like red sandstone and a gay, colourful style of dress he can't have changed since he was a boy. Local people whisper to me that he is eighty, which is absurd. He looks sixty and still rides to hounds whenever he gets a chance.

Percy has not been quite the same since he was 'nationalised,' as he is pleased to refer to his position under the new National Health scheme, and of course the change has been a sensational one from his point of view. After a lifetime of behaving like some benevolent and beloved Robin Hood, soaking his rich patients to pay for his poor ones, and preserving a religious impartiality in his treatment of disease wherever he found it, he awoke one July morning to discover himself a paid government clerk as well as an unpaid general practitioner. In fact, instead of having the one master in his sacred calling, he found he had two, and the second (who held the purse strings) was a vast, impersonal, remarkably uninformed machine with a predilection for having its million and one queries answered in triplicate. He says he's going to die of writer's cramp, but I think it is more likely to be apoplexy!

I suppose, in my more serious moments, I ought not to approve of him. He is obstinate and old-fashioned, hopelessly conventional and a snob. And yet, when science has let me down and a diagnosis is beyond me, when I've thought of everything and worked out everything and am still in the dark, he will shuffle up to the bedside, pull down an eyelid, sniff, and fish up out of some experience-taught subconscious an answer which is pure guesswork but which happens to be right.

Just then, as he came dancing in, I saw to my surprise that he was angry. His rather light brown suit was buttoned tightly round his

13

compact body, and his vivid blue eyes glared at me belligerently from his red face. He paused just inside the room and began to play with the coins in his trousers pockets.

'I suppose you're very pleased with yourself, Dr. Fowler.'

That 'Doctor' was a danger signal and I spoke cautiously.

'Not more than usual. What have I done now?'

He thrust his chin out at me. 'Over-conscientious, that's what's wrong with women in the professions. No thought of consequences. Lose a packet of aspirin and rush off to the police.'

'Oh,' I murmured, enlightened. 'The Dormital.'

'Dormital!' He repeated the word as though he had never heard of it, as perhaps he hadn't. 'What is it? One of these rubbishy phenobarbituric derivatives, I suppose. Where did you get it? Some darned silly firm send it to you as a sample?'

Since he had clearly been talking to Brush, our local Inspector, to whom I had reported everything, this was not too clever of him. Had he been a little less angry I might have pointed that out. As it was, I nodded.

'It's new. They've increased the solubility and—'

'Have they?' He could not have been more disgusted. 'Never dream of using that sort of

14

filth myself.'

I knew he was reputed never to prescribe anything save senna or old port and I nearly laughed.

'I'm sorry,' I murmured, 'but it is a poison, and I think someone really must have taken it out of my bag when I was on my round, so I reported it.'

At first I thought he was going to explode, but he thought better of it and I could see him making up his mind how he was going to manage me. Presently he disarmed me with a smile.

'I like a girl who stands up for herself,' he announced. 'You get that from your mother, no doubt.'

This time a grin did escape me. I had always suspected it was my mother's rather famous county family who had got me the job when Percy was checking my background. He shook his head at me then and asked me for the list of calls I had made on the day of the loss, and when I fetched it he went over each entry, calling everyone by his first name, which wasn't really surprising, perhaps, since he'd brought most of them into the world.

'Lizzie Luffkin,' he read aloud, putting a square forefinger on the page. 'Yes, I heard you'd been there. She's a strange old lady, Ann, rather a dangerous old lady. Makes up what she can't learn. Pity you called. Left the car in the road, I suppose? Unlocked?'

15

'I'm afraid so.'

'Don't blame you. Never locked a car in my life. Told Brush so. No, there's no one doubtful on this list, Ann. You couldn't have taken it with you.' He eyed me with a curious expression which was half shrewd and half obstinate. 'Make up your mind to that. You don't know Mapleford as I do. We're old-fashioned down here. Maybe we're even a little bit narrow. Am I making myself clear?'

'Not frightfully,' I said helplessly and he sighed.

'You're young, my dear. The people down here are not, and I'm not speaking of years. Brush and I have been discussing the matter and he agrees with me it would be very unwise to broadcast the loss. We don't want a lot of chatter in Mapleford about—well, to put it bluntly, about drugs.'

I gaped at him. To me all drugs are drugs, so to speak, dangerous or otherwise. I thought he was going to shake me.

'Veronal!' he exclaimed, making it sound like an improper word. 'Veronal, Ann. All your fancy barbituric fiddle-me-faddles are only veronal, and we've heard quite enough about *that* in our time.' He lowered his voice, although we were alone. 'The old Duke's sister died of it, poor wretched woman. She was an addict.'

Perhaps I was not as impressed as I ought to have been. I knew the Dukes of St. Pancras,

16

whose gothic towers overshadowed the little town, still dominated Mapleford minds, but the 'young Duke,' as he was called, had seemed on the elderly side to me.

'But *when* was all this?' I demanded.

Percy Ludlow met my eyes solemnly. 'Only thirty years ago,' he said without a tremor. 'No time at all in a place like this. I remember it as if it was last week. So do most other people. So you see, once we start muttering about lost or stolen veronal there'll be no end of talk. I know the people down here. Half of them have got nothing to do except chatter about their neighbours. You take my word for it, young woman, you'll have every maiden lady on your register suspected of taking narcotics if you're not very careful.'

It was a jolt to me. Although my intelligence told me he must be crazy, I knew in my heart that he was right. It was his famous trick of correct diagnosis all over again. I might be right in theory, but he knew the people of his funny little town.

'I'm terribly sorry,' I began, and he grinned at me.

'I hate scandal,' he remarked. 'In fact I'm terrified of it. I'll get you out of anything in Mapleford except scandal. Then I wouldn't lift a finger.' He shot one of his bright birdlike stares at me. 'What's your new friend at Peacocks like?'

That took me by surprise. It showed me,

17

too, what I ought to have known about the size and efficiency of Mapleford's espionage system. I had been down to Peacocks Hall exactly five times since old Mrs. Montgomery had let the house to Peter Gastineau in February. This man was one of my very few private patients—that is to say, one of those who, although they paid the compulsory weekly premium under the new scheme, elected to pay their doctor as well. That alone made him something of a rarity. I explained at once.

'Well, he's arthritic,' I said, 'and he had quite a "heart." He spent some time in a prison camp, and not one of the better ones either, by the look of him. He has a man and his wife looking after him.'

Ludlow grunted. 'All foreigners, I suppose?'

'Gastineau is naturalised but I imagine he's French- or Belgian-born. The servants aren't English either.'

'I see.' He seemed gloomy. 'I don't like foreigners. Pure prejudice, of course, but they all seem sly to me . . . all except the Americans and the Scots, and they've got other faults no doubt. What did Alice Montgomery want to let her house for?'

'She's gone to London for the spring.'

'Oh.' That cheered him. 'I didn't realise he hadn't come to stay.' He paused in his meanderings up and down the room and raised his eyebrows. 'Very lucky to let that old house for such a short time this weather. Why does a foreigner want to come down here in the cold? Darned damp hole to take his arthritis to, I should have thought. Well, I shouldn't see any more of him than you need, you know.'

He went off to the french windows but before he left glanced round.

'You're a bit too pretty with that black hair and blue eyes, and your figure's too good,' he said seriously. 'These old gals round here, they suspect that.'

(So it was Miss Luffkin, was it? Her little house was very near Peacocks. I might have known.)

'Those are faults I'll recover from with the years,' I said aloud.

'Eh? Oh yes, I suppose you will.' The notion did not appear to comfort him particularly. 'Goo'bye, my dear. Not another word about that other matter, mind. Leave that entirely to me.'

He went dancing off across the meadow like a gnome and as I watched him Rhoda came up behind me.

'I couldn't help hearing and it reminded me,' she said brazenly. 'This cottage is too small for secrets. That Mr. Gastineau rang up twice this morning. He's quite well but he wants to see you very urgently. Wouldn't leave a message.'

I could feel her curiosity bristling like a

hedgehog.

'He's well over forty and he's one of the ugliest men I've ever set eyes on,' I observed.

'Is he?' To my surprise she sounded quite relieved. As a rule any faint promise of romance sets her up for a week. I deduced that an arthritic foreigner was not acceptable, but as if she had been reading my mind she said suddenly: 'I've been remembering Mr. John, you see.'

So had I, of course. There are times when I find old Rhoda very nearly unbearable.

It was ten past five when I left the Cottage Hospital on the other side of the town and surgery was at six, but as I neared the lane which leads past Miss Luffkin's cottage to Peacocks Hall I thought I could just fit in a call on Mr. Gastineau. I was not going there because he attracted me irresistibly. He didn't. To my mind there was little that was entrancing about that battered and racked shell of a human being, but there was something there that I recognised and I thought I could sympathise with, and the interesting thing about it was that I couldn't give it a name. He and I shared a frame of mind, or I thought we did. There was something about his attitude towards life which struck a responsive chord in me. I could not define it. I had no idea what it was. It was an undercurrent, emotional and rather frightening, and it made me curious. I did not

20

even like him but I certainly wanted to know more about him.

Miss Luffkin was pruning the ramblers which grow over her hedge. As far as I know she never does anything else. Whenever I pass, be it winter or summer or merely the right time of year for pruning, there she is, secateurs in hand, snipping and brushing and tying and bending, while her quick eyes turn this way and that and her green gardening bonnet is never still.

I waved nonchalantly and sped by. I guessed she would stare after me and probably glance at her watch, so that later, when I came back, she could look at it again. It couldn't be helped.

Peacocks is one of those sprawling Elizabethan houses that seem to be nestling into the earth for warmth. As I pulled up, the front door creaked open and Gastineau himself appeared. He was delighted but also embarrassed to see me, I thought, and he came stiffly forward to open the car door.

'This is so kind that I am ashamed,' he said in his clipped, overprecise English as he led me into the house. 'I did not mean to drag you all the way out here. I merely have a little favour to ask, and I seem to be making all the trouble in the world.'

He glanced at me out of the corners of his dull black eyes and I thought again how extraordinarily ugly he was. He was a tall man

21

who was bent into a short one, and his skin was sallow and stretched over his bones. Worst of all, he gave one the impression that there had once been something vital and attractive about his looks, but that he was a ghost of himself and his deep-set eyes were without light.

I did not sit down. 'What can I do?' I enquired briefly. 'Surgery at six, and I've got to get back.'

He grimaced. 'Children with spots and old ladies with pains. An extraordinary life for such a pretty woman. But you like it, don't you?'

'I love it,' I admitted, 'and I'm afraid I never find it even distasteful.'

'I see you don't. You are more than clever, you are kind. That is more rare,' he said gravely. 'That is why I have turned to you. Doctor, I have to have an ambulance.'

It was so unexpected that I laughed and was sorry for it at once, he looked so worried.

'I realise I am being ridiculous,' he said slowly. 'I was they say—in a flat spin. A most awkward and difficult thing has happened and I have to do something about it. It is the widow of a very old friend and compatriot of mine. I have just heard that she is alone and ill in London. I fear she may be'—he hesitated and watched my face as he chose a word—'difficult, also.'

'Nerves?' I suggested. That was the usual story.

22

'It may be more than that.'

'Alcoholism?'

He threw out his stiff hands. 'I do not know. It is possible, anything is possible. All I can tell you is that I have to go to fetch her with an ambulance and to bring her here.'

I felt my eyebrows go up. I was beginning to learn that there is absolutely no depth of human folly to which the most unlikely patient will suddenly descend, but I was still green enough to venture a protest.

'It sounds a very tall order,' I began cautiously.

'Does it? It is all I can do.' He spoke with a queer obstinacy. 'I promised Maurice as he died that if there was ever anything I could do for Louise, I would. Now the moment has come and I must have her here.'

'It's a great responsibility.'

He turned on me. 'Please don't think I do not know. I have thought it out from every angle. For a week I have been deciding, but I know in my heart that I must bring her home. Radek and Grethe will look after her, and you, if you please, will come to see her and advise me. Then I shall know I have done what I could.'

He watched me to see if I was impressed, and I was of course. I was glad to see him taking so much interest in a fellow human being. I had not thought there was so much kindness or duty left in him. I only hoped he

23

knew what he was in for.

'I can order an ambulance for you,' I said gently. 'It only seems odd that her present doctor does not arrange it.'

'Ah, I was afraid you would notice that.' He smiled at me awkwardly. 'She has quarrelled with him, of course. There is nobody to look after her except the landlady, who says I must arrive with the ambulance. You will come with me, won't you, Doctor? You go to London on Saturdays.'

There I put my foot down. I was gentle, I hope, but firm. I could just see Percy's face if the 'foreigner' and I went gallivanting off to London in the local bone-wagon. Besides, he was asking too much. My Saturday trips to the capital were the week's one escape from Mapleford, and I felt my sanity depended on them. I was mildly surprised that he knew so much about my habits.

I could not dissuade him. 'But you could see her in London before she leaves.' He pleaded as though his life depended upon it, urgent as a child, his eyes two dusky holes in his head.

I weakened. I knew it was silly, but I did, and I turned to the open bureau in the corner to find a scrap of paper to write the address on. He nearly wept with gratitude as he dictated it to me.

I am certain I should never have noticed the scrap of blue tissue protruding from one of the tiny drawers which lined the desk if I had not

24

heard his sudden intake of breath and looked up just as he leaned past me to thrust the thing out of sight. As it was, I hardly saw it at all. I caught a glimpse of something which looked vaguely familiar and then there was nothing there save his twisted and stiffened hand, which was shaking violently.

When I glanced up at him in astonishment he was trying to laugh, but his eyes were anxious, I thought.

'It is a pigsty of a desk. That is what you are thinking, aren't you? Let me see what you have written. Yes, that's right. The name is Louise Maurice, the address 14 Barton Square. West 2.'

I was still rather surprised. I had plenty of patients who might have thrown a fit if I had lighted on an unpaid gas bill or an overdue demand for rates. Mapleford was full of them. But I did not think Gastineau was quite the type. I was fairly certain he had been genuinely alarmed and I wished I had seen the blue slip more closely. It had suggested something so familiar that I just could not place it.

My puzzled expression seemed to delight Peter Gastineau. He became quite lighthearted, suddenly, and insisted on seeing me to the car.

'I think I am a most brilliant judge of character,' he remarked unexpectedly as we shook hands in the drive. 'You are kind but you are also very practical, aren't you, and you

25

have a great sense of what is expedient.'

'I should be a menace as a doctor if I hadn't,' I said lightly, and climbed into the car.

'And you are not forgiving?' He had to raise his voice, since my foot was on the starter, and the effect was to make the question sound anxious and important. At the same moment I saw the clock on my dashboard and let in the clutch.

'I have a heart of flint,' I shouted over my shoulder as I shot away. It was only as I was waving to Miss Luffkin, who, as I had expected, was waiting in the dusk to see me go by, that it occurred to me that it was a most extraordinary remark for him to have made.

Percy was not on duty that night and when I got back there was a crowd at the surgery. The waiting room was packed and I cursed socialised medicine. To my mind its weakness was elementary and I felt somebody might have foreseen it. Since everyone was forced to pay a whacking great weekly premium for medical insurance, nearly everybody, not unexpectedly, thought they might as well get something out of it, and, as far as Mapleford was concerned, the three who stood between nearly everybody and the said something-out-of-it were Percy and his two assistants, who had not been exactly idle before.

Percy hired us a secretary, paying her out of the private fortune his wife left him, but she, poor girl, could not sign our names for us or

26

weigh up the merits of a claim, so the stream of importunates demanding free chits to the dentist, free wigs, postal votes, corsets, milk, orange juice, vitamin tablets, pensions, invalid chairs, beds, water-cushions, taxi rides to hospital, crutches, bandages, artificial limbs, and a thousand and one likely or unlikely requirements dogged us wherever we went. As Percy said, it was almost a relief to find someone who just had a pain.

To make matters more difficult, the more ignorant (and less sick) among the crowds had lost their old respect for our calling and treated us as if we were officials trying to cheat them out of their rights. However, I was not so dead against it all—except at surgery time—as was Percy. I thought I should probably learn some way of coping with it in the end, and meanwhile I strove to keep my mind clear and to remember at all costs that I was a doctor first and a form-filler second.

That night I worked until I was in a lather. The secretary was close on angry by the time I had finished and was taking a couple of minutes to listen to poor old Mr. Grigson's interminable tale of the strange noises his chest made in the night. He is a retired sea captain, full of years and dignity, and he had walked up to the surgery with his bronchitis because 'since he was not paying' me any more he did not like to drag me out to his cottage. I wished everyone was as thoughtful, but hoped

27

it had not killed him. In my gratitude and guilt I listened far too long, until the recital was ended abruptly by the telephone.

I fully expected the call to be from Rhoda, fuming over a spoiled meal, but I had been too sanguine. The message, uttered in a squeaky child's voice, was brief but explicit. Mrs. McFall had 'begun.' I took down my coat. Once Mrs. McFall 'began' it was time for all men of good will to get out the boats, man the defences, batten down the hatches, and call out the fire brigade, and the fault was not hers, poor fecund lady, but her husband's. Mrs. McFall had a fine baby every year and had been doing so with the beautiful regularity of sunrise or the autumnal equinox for as far back as anyone remembered. But Mike McFall, her truck-driving husband, had never got himself used to the phenomenon. Each essay into fatherhood came upon him as a new and terrible experience only to be endured with the help of alcohol in such vast quantities that the man was a raving lunatic throughout the whole affair.

Nurse Tooley ministered to the people in that area. She was a woman after my own heart. Her courage made me ashamed of my own and her endurance had to be observed to be credited. But even she felt Mrs. McFall's ever recurrent crises were two-woman jobs. I had promised her that if I was above ground the next time Mrs. McFall 'began' I would be

28

there.

'You deliver the child, Doctor,' she said, 'and I'll control himself.'

So I had to go.

It was dawn by the time we had finished. As the first cock crew the youngest McFall let out his first furious bellow at the world he had hardly inherited, poor chicken, and, soon after, a stalwart neighbour and her son agreed to take over the parents.

Nurse and I crept out into the grey light and because she was if anything even more weary than I we loaded her bicycle onto the car and I drove her home. Despite the hour, nothing would content her save that I step in for a cup of tea. Her round red face was full of anxiety.

'Sure I've got a little word I'd like to be saying to you, Doctor.'

I am easy, of course. Sometimes I hope it is not just weakness of character. I staggered in. The cottage was tiny and neat as a doll's house, and as Nurse Tooley scurried about putting out china I sat in the best chair and felt my eyelids grow sticky with sleep. There was something rather special about this woman, I thought idly as I watched her square energetic form, solid and strong as a cob pony. She was deft and shrewd and loyal, and the idea shot into my mind that when John and I got our children's clinic we should need her. In an instant I had remembered and the furious colour rushed into my face. It was the kind of idiotic trick my subconscious was always liable to play on me whenever I got overtired.

Nurse handed me a steaming cup and sat down beside me.

'You're done up. You look flushed,' she observed with concern. 'I ought not to have kept you out of your bed but I did want to speak to you. You're in trouble with the police, I hear.'

I blinked at her. 'I sent Sergeant Archer home with a chip on his shoulder after that accident on Castle Hill last week, if that's what you mean,' I said. 'He infuriated me. Fancy trying to get me to estimate if the dead driver had been drunk, there and then in the roadway! Especially as his hip flask had burst all over him.'

She shook her kind old head at my indignation.

'It's excited he was,' she said. 'But he's a bad enemy, Doctor, and you don't want enemies in the force, though God knows it's not my place to be mentioning it to you. No, I was wanting to enquire about this dangerous drug.'

That woke me up. I could just see what was happening now that Percy had decided to shut the stable door well after the horse had been stolen. I did my best to explain whilst keeping the irritation in my voice to a minimum.

'Dormital. Yes, I wrote it in my book as soon as Inspector Brush mentioned it to me.' Her Irish brogue was warm and deeply apologetic. 'He told me to keep it under my hat but to keep my eyes open for it just the same. You'll not have had it stolen, Doctor, not in Mapleford, for it's not at all useful. If it had been a nice sizeable packet of cascara, now, I wouldn't have trusted some of them. No, you've let it slip out of the car and someone has upped and slung it over the hedge. Could you tell me what it was like at all, for if it's found the chances are I shall be having it brought to me?'

I had described my loss carefully to the Inspector and I had no need to visualise it again.

'Why yes, I can,' I said. 'It was a white carton with some blue round the edges—a narrow band, I think. There was printing on the outside, just the usual details and guarantees. The carton had been opened and it held a two-ounce capsule bottle with the seal unbroken. Oh yes, and there was the ordinary literature inside, a flimsy, tightly printed blue paper . . .'

My voice dried suddenly as I heard my own words. A *blue* paper, tightly printed!

'What's the matter, Doctor?'

'Oh, nothing. Nothing of importance.' I managed to sound normal and to say good-bye and to get myself back into the car, but as I sped home through the half-awake streets it went through my mind like a little warning bell that perhaps I was making a silly mistake in

31

being so sorry for Gastineau and so ready to oblige him. The dreadful thing was that I could not be sure, yet it could have happened. I had not called at Peacocks Hall on the day I missed the Dormital, but I had seen Peter Gastineau. It was just after I had been to call on Miss Luffkin. I had left her safely in the house, for once, gargling her sore throat in the bathroom, and I came out to the car to find Gastineau standing beside it. I assumed he had just arrived after one of his little saunters down the road which were all the exercise he was able to take, but of course he might have been there much longer . . .

I was thinking about it as I reached my bed and fell asleep, and it was still in my mind when I woke a few hours later. The more I thought about it the more awkward it became, but at the same time my conviction that the blue paper was the same blue paper grew alarmingly. I half considered going to old Percy, and I think I would have done in the end had I not been so impossibly busy. As it was the only immediate effect of the whole incident was that I forgot to order the ambulance until I was in the midst of a strenuous afternoon at the Friday Welfare Clinic. I had to make the call from the phone on the desk and I remember thinking at the time that it was the most public telephone conversation I had ever had. Every mother and half the babies listened to me as if I was ordering a charabanc for an outing. There is not a lot of free entertainment in Mapleford and people certainly make the best of what there is. By nightfall everyone in the place would know of Gastineau's visitor, her name and where she came from and the exciting fact that I would see her in London, that fabulous city.

I don't know why it was, but I felt it was dangerous then.

Altogether it was a heavy week and on Saturday morning it was a thrill to put away my solid tweeds and climb into a silk suit and a squirrel cape, to put on a silly hat which made me look twenty again, and to drive off to the metropolis fifty miles away.

I had lunch at the Mirabelle with Edith Gower, an old buddy of mine. We had heavenly food and one of those gossips which are good for the soul. Afterwards we went to an exhibition of modern art and met two of her friends who had pictures there, so just for a little while I wallowed in a world as far away from Mapleford as it was possible to imagine. It did me no end of good.

It was a quarter before four before I realised it and I had to make a Cinderella exit and fly for Barton Square. It is no good pretending that I did not regret my promise to Peter Gastineau just then. I wished him and his poor Madame Maurice, if not at the bottom of the sea, at least in the middle of next week. They would wait for me, I had no doubt, but even so there was none too much time, as I had promised to have tea with Matron at St. James's at five.

I found Barton Square without much difficulty, and the narrow, slightly tattered grey houses rose up like a cliff above me as I crept round it looking for the number. To my astonishment there was no sign of the ambulance. I hoped they had not run into trouble on the road.

Number 14 was a surprise, too. For one thing, it was shut up like a Bedouin lady in walking-out costume. Drab curtains covered the windows and there appeared to be no lights behind them. It was one of those narrow slices of building with steps to the front door, and an area with a lion's cage of a railing round it. I went, up and rang the doorbell. I could hear its hollow clanging echoing through the hallway within, but there were no answering footsteps.

For some time I stood waiting, the cold wind whipping round me. Presently I rang again, and again I heard the bell, but still no one came. I was beginning to wonder if there could be two Barton Squares in the west of London when I thought I heard a movement in the basement below me. I suppose I had grown so used to admitting myself into patients' houses in Mapleford that I did not hesitate. I scrambled down the worn stone

34

steps of the area and, skirting the ashcan, entered the tiny porch which I found there. The inner door was closed and, after knocking without results, I tried it.

My hand was on the knob when a most disconcerting thing happened. It turned in my fingers as someone grasped it on the other side, and the door jerked open, pulling me in with it so that I finished up with my nose less than six inches from another face immediately above me.

'Oh,' I said inadequately.

To do him justice, the stranger seemed quite as startled as I was. He was a tall middle-aged man with a gentle, vague expression. His good brown suit was loose for him and he clutched a well-brushed hat and a carefully rolled umbrella. Just now he was hesitating, waiting for me to speak first.

I must have been rattled, I suppose, for I said the first thing that came into my head. I said: 'Have you seen the ambulance?'

The question shocked him. I saw his eyes flicker and he said in a quiet, pleasant voice which yet matched his vague expression: 'Oh, there was an ambulance, was there? Oh dear.'

I am afraid I am one of those people who can't help going to the assistance of the socially put out. Although I was halfway into someone else's house, and in the wrong if anyone was, I felt I ought to help him, he looked so worried.

'I'm Dr. Fowler,' I explained. 'I've come to see a patient who, I understand, is to be taken into the country by ambulance. Her name is Maurice. Is this the right house?'

He peered at me in what seemed to be distress, and it occurred to me that I must make a rather odd sort of Doctor in my all too feminine clothes, but apparently he did not doubt me.

'Do you know, I really can't tell you,' he said at last, adding sincerely, 'I'm so sorry. No one seems to be in the house at all except—well, perhaps you wouldn't mind coming to see for yourself?'

He turned, and, highly mystified, I followed him into a labyrinth of those gloomy dungeons and subdungeons which our ancestors were pleased to call 'domestic quarters.'

The first, which was unfurnished as well as deserted, led to a second, smaller room fitted up snugly enough as a kitchen. There, stolidly eating her tea and toast, as if no one had been ringing a bell or standing on a doorstep, was a large clean elderly woman with the eyes and jaw movement of a cow in a field. She looked up as we appeared, smiled pleasantly, and just went on eating. It was, I think, the most unnerving welcome I have ever received.

As soon as I attempted to speak to her the mystery was solved. Still smiling, but with the complete indifference of one who knows something is hopelessly beyond her, she shook

36

her head and, with a forefinger, pointed first to one ear and then to the other. She was stone deaf, poor soul.

I opened my bag and was ferreting round in it for a pencil when a voice murmured in my ear.

'Well, you know, I fear that's no good,' muttered the man with the umbrella. 'She doesn't read English. I tried that.'

'What nationality is she?'

'That's it, I can't find out.' He sounded as helpless as I felt, and added as if he thought I ought to have an explanation, 'I just happened to call, you see.'

I didn't quite, as it happened, but it was the woman I was interested in. At that moment she broke the silence. After taking a draught from her cup, which looked as if it contained something boiling, she wiped her mouth and, leaning back in her chair, spoke in the very loud toneless voice of one who cannot hope to hear.

'All gone.' Her accent was unrecognisable and I could only just understand her. 'All gone.' She smiled again. 'No one.' She was trying hard and her hands illustrated the emptiness of the house above us.

'Where?' I was trying her with lip language and she watched me carefully but shook her head. It was frightful. We were two intelligences with no hope of communication.

'Who?' I tried again and she laughed.

I smiled back and shrugged my shoulders. There was nothing to do but go away and I had turned when her unnatural bellow filled the room again.

'Sick woman,' she shouted.

I swung round eagerly and nodded to show we were on the right track.

'Yes,' I agreed. 'Yes. Where?'

She sat thinking. I could see her doing it, her broad forehead wrinkled and her eyes moving. Once or twice she began to frame a word, but it was not an English one I thought, and she always rejected it. Presently she rose and pushed back the chair.

'A-a-ah,' she began cautiously. 'Sick woman. Morter. Morter . . .'

'Motor,' muttered the man at my side. 'I think she means "motorcar".'

I nodded at the woman, who smiled, well pleased.

'Morter . . . whoosh . . . gone. Sick woman gone.' She sank down once more and pulled her plate towards her. We might not have been there.

The man with the umbrella accompanied me to the door, getting there first to hold it open for me.

'Dr. Fowler,' he began, giving me a tremendous start because I had forgotten that I had introduced myself, 'there was a cream ambulance coming out of the square just as I came in.'

'Really? When was this?'

He considered. 'Now let me see. Yes. Yes, it must be just over an hour ago.' He was not at all happy and his discomfort was nearly as evident to me as my own. 'It was caught up in the traffic,' he continued casually, 'and I happened to notice that it came from a place called Mapleford. Would that be the one, Doctor?'

'Yes,' I said absently. 'Yes, that's it. I wonder . . .'

I don't know what made me glance squarely at him at that particular moment, but I did, and what I saw set me back squarely on my heels. All the vagueness had vanished from his pale eyes and for a split second they were shrewd and hard and frighteningly intelligent. The next moment he was his old, apologetic helpless self again, but I was frightened and I bade him good afternoon and hurried off up the area steps, feeling almost panicky.

Before I drove off to see Matron at St. James's I spoke to the officer on point duty, and he confirmed that an ambulance had called on that side of the square at about three o'clock.

I was furious. By that time I was disgusted with the whole business and there is one unalterable rule for a doctor who begins somewhat belatedly to scent mystery: that is for him to wash his hands of the affair as quickly and thoroughly as possible. I put the whole business firmly out of my mind and did not think of it again until nearly half past eleven that evening when I was driving home. By that time I was better-tempered. The night was glorious and I had time to think. I decided to give Gastineau and his lady friend a rest for a bit. It would be quite easy for me to plead overwork and get young Dr. Wells, Percy's other assistant, to take them over for a while.

By the time I turned into the familiar road I had almost forgotten Gastineau and I saw the lights on in the cottage with dismay. Rhoda never stays up for me when I go to town. She goes to the cinema first and then to bed. She leaves me a jug of milk and a biscuit on the table, and sometimes a few enlightening remarks scribbled on the pad. If she was still up, something very unusual must be afoot.

I left the car just outside the garage and sneaked in by the back door. Rhoda was in her basket chair, knitting furiously to keep herself awake. As I appeared she glanced up and put a finger on her lips.

'Who?' I whispered.

'He won't go.' She nodded at the inner door and, taking up a final stitch, rolled up the vest she was making. 'It's that foreigner,' she murmured. 'He came creeping in just as I was going to bed. Said he'd been trying to telephone here all the evening and just had to come and see you to satisfy himself.' She paused, her bright eyes meeting mine. 'I can't

40

say I think much of him now I've seen him.'

'Nor do I,' I agreed, keeping my voice down. 'Why didn't he go to Dr. Wells?'

'Oh, he wouldn't. He said it was personal.' She was watching me with the suspicion of a mother, ready to defend but prepared for the worst.

'Rubbish,' I declared wholeheartedly. 'I'll go and send him home. I've never heard such nonsense.'

Her pink face cleared. 'That is a weight off my mind,' she said unnecessarily. 'I couldn't see what you saw in him. Besides, I've had a letter today from Southersham. It came by the second post and there's real news in it. Something *you'll* never guess.'

I am afraid I interrupted her. Rhoda would pause for a good gossip if the house was on fire. Just then my mind was occupied. This development was more than I had bargained for.

'I suppose you do mean Mr. Gastineau?'

'That's what he called himself.' She conveyed it was probably a pseudonym. 'If you can get rid of him, it's more than I could without taking my strength to him. Go and try. I'll pop the kettle on, and when you come back I'll tell you my bit of news if you're in a better temper.'

Peter Gastineau was sitting by the fire, his elbows on his knees and his long hands drooping between them. He got up stiffly when he saw me and took a step forward. He was struggling with nervous excitement and his black eyes had a light in them I had not seen before.

'I wouldn't have had this happen for the world,' he began. 'Doctor, you must be so angry.'

'Not at all.' I was not so inexperienced that I was going to let the party become in any way emotional. 'I am very tired, I am afraid, but is there anything I can do?'

'I hope so.' He spoke fervently. 'I am in a dreadful predicament. I am so frightened that I have made a most serious mistake.' He sat down again without being asked and I noticed a blue line round his mouth. 'I tried to catch you this morning, when I heard from London of the change of plan. You'd gone, of course.' He was not apologising so much as stating the case, and I had the wind taken out of my sails.

'I gathered that the patient was removed earlier in the afternoon,' I observed acidly, and at once he was interested and even excited.

'Oh, you did see someone, did you? That is good. Who did you find there?'

'A deaf woman and a man who was visiting her. What happened exactly?'

He did not reply directly. The discovery that I had not merely found the door shut in my face seemed to engross him.

'If you saw somebody, made yourself known to them, that's something.' He spoke with

42

relief and I found myself peering at him. He had changed somehow. There was something new about him and to my annoyance I could not decide what it was. I wondered if he was stewing up for a nerve crisis. He caught my expression and pulled himself together. 'I am almost beside myself,' he explained awkwardly. 'As you know, since . . . since the war I have become such a lover of comfort and order and peace. Any change of plan makes me jitter. This morning the good woman who has been looking after Madame Maurice telephoned to say that the hour of departure must be changed. I was in despair, you were in London and out of reach. Finally I got hold of the ambulance people and with some difficulty got them to go earlier.'

He took a deep breath and leant back. The idea, apparently, was that I should sympathise with him.

'Well, if you got her here, that's all right,' I said soothingly. 'There was no need for you to come up here tonight.'

He opened his eyes wide. 'But I came to fetch you. You must see her.'

'Not tonight,' I said firmly 'That's out of the question. It's very late. Far better let her sleep now and I'll come round in the morning.'

He seemed astounded. I saw a glimpse of something in his face which startled me. I thought he was going to rave at me. It was a queer expression, very fleeting and familiar. I

43

have seen it on the faces of tiny boys when they are suddenly deprived of something they want very much. It is elemental rage, I suppose. Anyhow he controlled it and said meekly enough:

'She is so strange. Neither Grethe nor I know what is wrong. It is a great responsibility.'

'Have you taken her temperature?'

'Grethe tried. It was impossible.'

'Is she delirious?'

'I am not sure.'

I put my temper under hatches. Here was a fine household to undertake the care of an invalid.

'Then you should have gone to Dr. Wells, but it's too late now, I'm afraid. Look here, would you like to ring your housekeeper now and see how she is?'

He shook his head. 'You must come back with me.' He paused and added devastatingly, 'Without you I cannot very well get home. I made certain you would come and so I sent my man back with the car. We could try to telephone for a taxi, I suppose.'

Now that was a trump card, had he known it. I could just see myself waking up old Chatterbox at the local garage and getting him to turn out to take Gastineau away from my house at midnight on my day off duty. I began to feel very angry indeed.

'Very well,' I said. 'Put on your coat and I'll

run you back and take a look at her.' There was nothing else I could trust myself to say.

I got my own heavy tweed from the lobby and took him out through the kitchen to the yard. Rhoda gaped at me and I let them both see that I was not exactly pleased.

On the journey I said nothing at all, as far as I remember. After one or two ineffectual attempts to interest me in my new patient, he gave up and we raced on in silence.

There was a light in Miss Luffkin's front room which went out as we sped past, and I was unreasonably glad that the night had become so dark. All the lights were on at Peacocks. The old house looked as though it were celebrating something. Grethe, the housekeeper, a swart eastern European with the most eager eyes I have ever seen in a woman, met us in the hall. She spoke to Gastineau in a language I didn't even recognise and he turned to me.

'Madame Maurice is in the guest room. Will you come up?'

'Yes, I'll see her since I'm here,' I agreed ungraciously, but I did not take my coat off.

I followed him up the polished staircase, which was black with age and very wide, on to a large landing where Radek was waiting. I got the impression that this solid wedge of a man, with the heavy face and coarse yellow hair, had been sitting outside one of the doors, but I could not be sure. He too said something to his employer and Gastineau nodded and signalled to him to leave us.

'She's here,' he said, and without knocking opened a door on the extreme right of the landing, facing the back of the house.

I went in first. It was one of those tremendous rooms which were designed to house a family. There was a coal fire in the grate and not much other light, and at the end of the plane of carpet I could see a big old-fashioned tester bed with a canopy and chintz hangings.

Two things impressed me the moment I entered. One was that the patient, whatever was wrong with her, was snoring more or less normally, and the other that there was a violent smell of alcohol in the room. I think I was saved from turning to box Gastineau's ears by the recollection of the story which little Mr. Featherstone, the vet, had told me the week before. He said his Christmas evenings were always spoiled by dowagers who sent for him to see their apparently-dying pets, and were furious when he had to tell them that if they fed a dog on plum pudding and brandy sauce they must not be surprised if they became tipsy.

I went over to the bed and looked down. It was so dark that I could only make out a little face and a cloud of hair on the pillow. I spoke without looking up.

'May I have some more light, please?'

'Of course.' His voice sounded odd, husky with intense excitement. I was concentrating on the patient at the time and although I noticed it I did not pay much attention to it until afterwards. He had gone round to the other side of the bed and now turned an unusually powerful reading lamp on the two of us. It almost blinded me. I waved it down a bit.

The woman lying before me was scarcely thirty and must, I reflected, be quite beautiful when her face was less flushed and her mouth less slack. Her fair hair was bleached but very lovely and it spread round her head on the pillow like a halo. I don't know if I am particularly stupid or unobservant, but I do know that my training has taught me to concentrate only on certain details of a patient's face. It has happened that I have not recognised a woman whom I have been treating for weeks when I have met her some time later in the street. Anyhow, I know that on that night, up in the vast guest room at Peacocks, it was fully five minutes before the message which was hammering on the back of my mind suddenly got through my professional concentration and I looked at the woman and realised who she was.

Francia Forde.

I had never studied her photographs consciously and I had never seen her films, but now that I was confronted by her I knew it was she as surely as if I had lived with her half my

47

life. In one way I suppose I had. It was one of those revelations which are at once terrifying and shaming. I saw just how much and how minutely I must have thought about her, and just how avidly my subconscious mind must have seized on every little trick and detail of her face.

I found I knew the moulding of her cheek and the faint hollow beside her temples as well as I knew the lines round Rhoda's mouth. There were differences I hadn't expected, tiny blemishes the camera had not shown. This woman had not been doing herself much good just recently. There was a network of tiny lines, finer than a spider's web, on her eyelids. But she was still lovely. So lovely that the old helpless feeling settled down over my heart without my daring to question why or whence it came.

It was some seconds before I realised that I was being watched from the other side of the bed and I wondered if I could have given myself away. Gastineau couldn't have known anything about my private life, whatever the explanation of Francia Forde's appearance in his house might be. That was one thing I was certain of.

Fortunately I have a poker face by nature and my training has strengthened the gift. If I am scared or even very interested I am mercifully merely liable to appear preoccupied, and when he said at last, 'Well,

48

Doctor?' I felt sure he had noticed nothing.

I returned to my job with relief, remembering that it was nothing to do with me who the woman was or why she was there. All I had to decide was what was wrong with her. That was not very difficult. She showed no inclination to awake, but she was by no means unconscious and when I shook her gently she flung away from me with an incoherent word.

'Was she like this when you collected her this afternoon?' I enquired.

'Not so sleepy.' He sounded doubtful and I wondered whether he could be really so stupid as he appeared to be.

'Yes, well,' I said 'she's been taking a considerable amount of some sort of sedative, which you will probably find among her luggage if you look, and to put it bluntly she has also had a great deal of alcohol. You will doubtless find the source of that too if you use your eyes.'

I was falling back on an excessive formality because I was both annoyed and shaken.

'I should look under the bed valance, behind the curtains, and of course in her suitcases.'

He nodded. He was not going to pretend complete ignorance, I was glad to see.

'I can hardly believe it,' he said, coming round the bed and walking down the wide room with me. 'It doesn't seem possible. She's a very fine actress, you know.' He shot a little quizzing glance at me on the last word or two, but I was in an odd emotional state just then and I didn't want to discuss her, or even to find out if I was right about her identity. I just wanted to get out of that dreadful room.

'Really?' I sounded uninterested. 'Well, I'm afraid I can't help her any more. Take away any alcohol or any drugs you may find. Give her bismuth or something of the sort in the morning, and if she is very excitable, one ounce and no more of whisky at eleven. By tomorrow night you should know whether the trouble is—er—chronic or not.'

To my discomfort I heard him laugh very softly.

'You're very businesslike.'

'I'm also very tired. Perhaps you'll forgive me if I get away now.'

I moved towards the door and he came after me.

'When will you come again?'

'You may not need me any more,' I said cheerfully. 'There's nothing very wrong with her now. This may not be a regular thing. But if it is, you'll need rather different advice from any I could give you. Good night, Mr. Gastineau. No, don't come down. I can find my way out.'

He hobbled to the stairhead with me and looked down as I descended. I heard his murmur just above me and the words were so extraordinary that I thought I must have mistaken them.

'Courage,' I thought I heard him say half to himself and half to me. 'That was the only thing I doubted.'

I glanced up sharply but he was simply smiling and nodding.

'Good night, Doctor. It was very good of you. Thank you. Good night.'

I did not realise I was so shaken by the whole business until I got out into the air. As my hands gripped the steering wheel I found they were trembling. This alarmed me as much as anything, for my life is based on the premise that I am a sensible, unshockable sort of person. I am one of those who have never thought mystery, doubt or drama in any way exciting. I hate the lot of them. My instinct is to scramble stolidly to my feet whatever happens to me, like one of those toys which are weighted at the bottom, and the result is that I seldom get rattled and am made twice as bad by noticing it when I do.

As soon as I got the car going it occurred to me very forcibly that if Gastineau's Madame Maurice was really Francia Forde (I admitted there was a strong chance I had made a crazy mistake here) there was something very odd indeed about her arrival in Mapleford, and the sooner I made a graceful escape from the affair the better.

I was reflecting on the most practical way of arranging this, and was thinking that Wells would be a more sympathetic ally than Ludlow, when I was pulled up by someone who walked out into the road and waved a torch at me. I trod hard on the brakes before I realised that I was just outside Miss Luffkin's house.

There she was, wrapped up like a bundle of laundry, her thin excited face peering out at me from under a sou'wester tied on with a Liberty scarf.

'Oh, Doctor, it *is* you.' I was aware of her eyes noting that I was hatless and had a silk suit on under my ulster. 'I've been so worried about those poor people down at Peacocks. I saw the ambulance go by. Is someone very bad, Doctor?'

I have sometimes thought that Lizzie Luffkin's curiosity is quite as pathological as her popeyes, an overactive thyroid gland. I don't believe she can help it. Even she must have known that the solicitude in her voice was unconvincing. The sight of the ambulance must have acted like a red rag to a bull on her, and not knowing the explanation for five or six hours had been pure agony.

'Nothing serious,' I said with forced heartiness. 'Just an old friend of Mr. Gastineau's come to convalesce.'

'Oh, I see, a friend.' Her disappointment was so obvious that it was funny. She clung to the door of the car, eager for just a scrap more gossip. 'You are out very late, Doctor.'

'Yes, I am, aren't I?' I shouted above the engine I was revving. 'But so are you. Good night.'

I shot away into the darkness, hoping I had not been too abrupt and should pay for it. In ten minutes I was home and I put up the car and walked into the kitchen. If Rhoda was sometimes a thorn in my flesh, there was nothing like that about her now. She was the one person in the whole world whom I knew to be unshakably on my side. As always, whenever I needed a really sober-minded confidante, she was there.

I told her who I thought was at Peacocks Hall. I can see her now turning away from the stove, the kettle in one firm red hand. There was no smart comeback, no undue surprise.

'Are you sure?'

'No, and I can't believe it. It's too ridiculous. Have you got that photograph you were showing me the other day?'

She got it for me at once out of her own private drawer, the middle one of the dresser, and spread it on the table for me to see.

I stood looking at it carefully for some time. I could see where it had been touched up, where the line of the jaw had been sharpened and the eyelashes drawn in. But the other facts were all there. It was not a usual face, not even one of a type. The contours were definite and convincing, the features line for line the same.

'Is it?' Rhoda came to stand beside me and

put a heavy hand on my shoulder, a possessive gesture she seldom permits herself.

'I think it is,' I said slowly. 'It's either her or a double. It's not sense, though, Rhoda. How could she be here, calling herself Maurice?'

'*He's* calling her Maurice,' she corrected me with typical reasonableness. 'Besides, it's not quite so funny as you seem to think. You've not seen the paper today, have you?' She was ferreting under the radio table, where she keeps current reading matter, as she spoke, and soon came back with a copy of her favourite daily. 'I noticed this when I was reading at lunchtime.'

It was a small news item, one of those four-line affairs tucked into the foot of a column.

STAR TO REST. Friends of Miss Francia Forde, the screen actress, say that the star is to take a few days' complete rest in the country after the ardours of making still pictures for the 'Moonlight Girl,' a new advertising campaign due to begin in the press on Monday.

I read it through two or three times before it made any sense to me.

'That's all very well,' I began at last. 'But I don't see why she should come down here in an ambulance. I don't see why Gastineau should tell me this Maurice story or why she should be staying with them.'

'Perhaps she's hiding.'

'Who from? She's very well known but she's not one of the American top-liners. There aren't armies of fans hounding her.'

Rhoda had become very thoughtful. If I had been more myself I should have noticed that tightening of the lips and the lowering of the thick determined brows, and might have been on guard.

'You're not satisfied, are you?' she enquired, and the slightly hopeful note in her tone irritated instead of warning me.

'Well, of course I'm not,' I burst out angrily. 'How can I be? I'm persuaded to send an ambulance to London to fetch a woman who appears to be no more than very tipsy, and when I see her I recognise her as . . . well, as somebody other than the person she is represented to me to be.'

'Ah,' said Rhoda, taking a beaker from the dresser with the idea of pouring us a hot drink to take to bed, 'you are like your father when you talk like that. I can hear him this minute. My word, he'd be wild!'

'The extraordinary thing is that she should come *here*,' I went on, ignoring the reference to Father, although it had its comforting side.

She paused, jug in hand, and turned a pink face to me.

'Coincidences do happen. That's life. I've seen it a hundred times. Some people call it fate and some people call it religion, but

55

whatever it is there's no denying it happens.'

I always find Rhoda rather difficult to bear when she gets on this theme. It is one of her favourites and there is no stopping her. I took up my beaker and edged for the door.

'You can run,' she said warningly, 'you can run, but it'll catch you. This is a coincidence, and it's more of a one than you know. You get some sleep.'

In my ignorance I felt that this last remark of hers was the only one that contained any reason at all, and I went off to bed feeling that at least there was solace there.

Despite my worries, I felt the slow anaesthesia of sleep creeping over me the moment I pulled up the blankets. Just before I slid away into unconsciousness I remembered two things. The first was that I had not asked Rhoda what news the letter from our old home had brought her, and the second that in my preoccupation with the patient I had not tackled Gastineau about the scrap of blue paper I thought I had seen on his desk. Even in my drowsing state this last seemed a formidable proposition and I sailed away into oblivion without making up my mind how to tackle it.

The next day began quite normally for a Sunday. That is, I was up very late and only partially by mistake. I fear I leave the worst of my paperwork—and there is no end to it in these days—to Sunday morning, and I settled down to a mountain of hospital reports on patients I had sent there, about a quarter to eleven. I had not forgotten Francia Forde by any means, but I was trying to get her out of my mind. It was not just Francia. She brought back too many unbearable memories altogether. I was still stunned by the knowledge that she had got so close to me.

The only unusual element that morning was provided by Rhoda. Once or twice I wondered if she was ill. She bustled about as if she was thinking of spring cleaning, and for ten minutes we had a wrangle because she objected to my clothes. I was very comfortable in slacks and a twin set, and her remarks on my 'slovenliness' and my 'nice new red wool upstairs' completely bewildered me. In the end I got the better of her by insisting on taking her temperature. It was normal but her pulse was slightly quick, and I recommended a sedative. She left me alone after that but I heard her go out to the back gate several times, which was puzzling, for no one goes calling in Mapleford on a Sunday.

The sound of the car pulling up in the road outside filled me with sudden apprehension that Gastineau had come for me again. He seemed to have no idea that a doctor might have any hours. Also I guessed that his patient, if not in any danger, might well be feeling pretty sick by this time.

I got up and tiptoed across the room to peer

57

out of the small window overlooking my minute front garden, so that I should get fair warning.

I pulled the curtain back half an inch and the next moment stood petrified, every nerve in my face tingling as if I had pressed it to a network of live wires.

John Linnett was standing at the small iron gate.

For a long minute I simply did not believe it. I watched him hesitate, glance nervously at the cottage, and then fumble with the latch through his heavy driving glove.

He looked much older and there was a touch of apprehension in his expression which I had never seen there before. It may sound absurd to say so, but I knew it really was John because of the changes in him.

The car he had come in, a low roadster covered with dust, stood in the lane behind him, empty, so he was alone. Of course. The explanation of his sudden arrival broke over me like a wave. He had come to find me because Francia was at Peacocks, and I was supposed to be attending her. My scattered wits came together with a jerk. I felt my expression setting and becoming hard and brittle and very bright. If I had had any sense at all, I suppose, I should have expected him to appear on the scene sooner or later.

I threw open the window at once. 'Hallo, John.'

'Ann.' He came stamping over the garden, his coat skirts flying and his hands outstretched. I saw how thin he was, suddenly, and how the bones of his face stood out. 'My dear girl, thank God you're all right.'

It was the most unlikely and most unexpected approach, and it floored me as nothing else would have done. He took my hands through the window and looked anxiously into my face.

'What's happened? What's the matter? I came at once, of course.'

The whole thing was beyond me. My new hard cheerfulness cracked completely. I was only aware that he was there, trying to get into the house, and, apparently, through the window.

Rhoda opened the front door. I heard her say something to him and the next moment he was in the room, filling it. The nervous energy which I remembered in him so well had become intensified. His narrow eyes were eager and still terribly anxious.

'You look all right,' he said with relief. 'You haven't altered at all. In fact you're better. Lost your puppy fat. What is it, Ann? What's happened? I got the telegram early this morning and I've been driving ever since.'

There was a passage of stupefied silence from me, and a movement from Rhoda lurking in the doorway.

'I sent it.' Her tone was flat and her face

expressionless, save for a faint gleam of belligerence in her eye. 'I put your name, Miss Ann, because I thought that Mr. John might not remember mine. As soon as you came in last night and said you weren't satisfied I knew it was my duty.'

The barefaced wickedness of it took my breath away, but the thing that foxed me utterly was how she'd known where to send. She answered that one as if I'd asked the question.

'I got a letter yesterday from my niece in Southersham. I was going to tell you about it but you were too busy to listen. She told me that they'd heard down there that Mr. John was attached to the hospital at Grundesberg in Northamptonshire, so last night, when you'd gone to bed, I got on the telephone and sent a telegram to him there.'

I said nothing. There was nothing to say. She gave me a defiant stare and opened the door.

'I've got the lunch to see to,' she said as if I was thinking of disputing it. 'I'm doing something special because I expected Mr. John. You still care for pancakes, I expect, sir?'

'I do,' he said without thinking and returned to me. His expression was not only anxious now, but somehow frightened. 'I thought *you* sent,' he said. 'I thought *you* wanted me for something. The telegram just said, "I think you had better come at once, Ann Fowler," and gave the address.'

It was his dismay that got me. The utter disappointment came out so clearly that if I had been only half as sensitive where he was concerned it would have reached me. I found I knew him as if he had never been away.

'If you've driven from Grundesberg this morning you must be exhausted,' I said hastily. 'Sit down and I'll get you a drink. We'll thrash this out in a minute.'

He laughed and it was a laugh I had known from childhood.

'I haven't even shaved. The thing got me out of bed at dawn. What's the mystery? What aren't you satisfied about?'

I had my back to him, since I was fixing a highball on the sideboard.

'Rhoda got scared by something I said last night,' I began with a casualness which was not convincing even to me. 'I was called out to a new patient and she turned out to be . . . Francia Forde.'

'Oh.' His disinterest was startling 'Is she down here? I thought I read somewhere that she was setting up as an advertising model.'

I swung round to look at him blankly and he took the glass from my hand.

'I've not seen her in four years,' he said slowly. 'I shouldn't get involved in any of her machinations if I were you, Ann. She's a dangerous piece of work.'

I don't drink whisky as a rule but I had

poured a highball for myself and now, in sheer absent-mindedness, I swallowed it almost whole, nearly choking myself. I had tears in my eyes and was gasping for breath and I said the first thing that came into my head.

'John, what happened to you?'

He met my eyes steadily but he was ashamed, even frightened, and desperately miserable.

'God knows, Ann.'

That was all, but I knew about it suddenly, or I knew a very great deal.

Rhoda came in to set lunch at that juncture. She was very busy being the model housekeeper, keeping her eyes downcast and wearing the wooden expression of one who has withdrawn completely from any awkward situation she may have precipitated.

Because I wanted to talk to him so badly and found it so easy I asked John about Grundesberg.

'Understaffed and overcrowded. The usual story in that kind of district,' he said easily. 'Just the place to catch up on one's general work. I've been there nearly eighteen months, ever since I was demobbed.'

'But I thought . . .' I began before I could stop myself, 'I mean I thought you came out in '45.'

'No,' he said coolly. 'I got some extended leave then and set about making a goddam fool of myself in a pretty big way, but after that

I sneaked back into the army and went to the Far East.'

'Hence—the silence,' I murmured.

He said nothing at all. He did not even look at me. Rhoda saved us by a remarkable entrance, the silver soup tureen which we never use held high.

That meal was a revelation to me. I knew she had her secret store cupboard stocked against Christmas (or another war, perhaps) but I had no idea that it could produce anything like that. She waited on us, too, putting on a remarkable act which was part Maître of the Ritz and part Nanny at the party.

John began to enjoy himself. I had seen it happen to him so often in our childhood. The prickles drew in and the silences grew fewer. He began to laugh and to tease us both indiscriminately. No one mentioned the telegram. I think we forgot it deliberately. This was a dispensation, a time of sanctuary, something that might never come again.

After the meal we sat by the fire while the shadows grew long outside. There was so much to tell about the present that there was no need to speak of anything else, and we were chattering, and eating some filberts which Rhoda produced, as contentedly as if we were back in my schoolroom at Southersham.

I spoiled it. We were talking of his life in Grundesberg and he was giving me a highly comic if horrific description of the lodgings he shared with the other house surgeon when I said suddenly and without any excuse at all:

'Are you still married to that woman, John?'

It was like breaking a gaily coloured bubble. The light went out in our little make-believe Sunday afternoon of a world.

'Yes,' he said, and added flatly, 'I suppose so.'

I said nothing more and after a long time he began to talk. At first I hardly heard what he was saying because I had made the panic-stricken discovery that his being there made the kind of difference to my life that colour makes to a landscape. It made it sense. I had never before dared let myself believe that that could happen.

'If I stop telling you I shall stop making excuses for myself,' he was saying, 'and there aren't any. When I realised exactly what I had done, I decided that I was mental and I went right away. I meant to stay away, and I did . . .' He turned on me with sudden anger. 'Damn you, Ann. I was all right until I got that telegram.'

'So was I.' It slipped out before I could stop it.

I could hear the words breaking like a little crystal dish on stone.

He lunged clumsily out of his chair and caught me as I sat, pushing his rough cheek into my neck and holding my shoulder blades with heavy, well-remembered hands. There was no helping it, no stopping it. I put my hands into his hair and held him close while my heart healed.

*   *   *

Percy Ludlow had to tap at the french windows twice before we heard him at all. The room was fairly dark but he is not exactly blind and he was pink and apologetic when at last I got over there to admit him.

He had walked across the meadow with a packet of the endless papers which dogged our existence and at first he was disposed to thrust them at me and depart, but I forced him to come in and be introduced.

'This is Dr. Ludlow, John,' I said. 'I told you, I'm his assistant. And this is Dr. Linnett, Dr. Ludlow. We were brought up together in Southersham.'

Percy gave me one of his sidelong glances.

'I formed the impression that you were old friends,' he said primly. 'I can't think why I haven't heard of you before, young man. She's a very close young woman, Dr. Fowler, almost secretive.'

I thought that at any moment he was going to enquire how long 'this' had been going on, but I got him into a comfortable chair and was on the point of seeing about some tea when Rhoda came in without ceremony.

'You didn't hear the phone, did you?' she

65

said. 'It's the gentleman from Peacocks, and that you must go down to see her. He said he'd come for you if he didn't hear.'

'Eh, what's that? Is that the foreigner?' Percy startled Rhoda, who had not seen him.

'Mr. Gastineau.' I glanced sharply at John to see if he would recognise the name, but clearly it meant nothing to him. He was standing in front of the fire with his chin up and the most obvious and reckless expression of delight in his eyes.

Percy grunted. 'A woman down there now?' he enquired.

'I understand it's a Madame Maurice,' I explained cautiously. 'He brought her from London yesterday and fetched me up late to look at her. My impression was that she was mainly tipsy.'

'More than probable.' He jerked his chin up to show his complete distrust of all the millions in the world who had not got themselves born as close to Mapleford as possible. 'Perhaps you'd better run down, though, eh?'

This was just like him. He would reproach me for visiting Peacocks at all and then insist that I answer the first telephone call at speed. It irritated me because I had been expecting Gastineau to ring all day, and, since I was convinced that there was no one very ill there, I was going to cajole Wells to take the call for me. Wells is an outspoken young man and I felt he might do everybody a bit of good. Percy made all this impossible. I knew once I started to explain he would infer that Gastineau had been making passes at me, and nothing I could say would convince him otherwise.

Rhoda piled on the agony by remarking that the 'foreign gentleman' wouldn't take no for an answer.

Percy nodded to me. 'You change into a Christian skirt and pop down and settle the trouble,' he said cheerfully. 'Dr. Linnett and I will have a smoke until you come back. It won't take you ten minutes.'

I have given up wondering at Percy's impudence. I knew he was dying to get the lowdown on what he clearly thought was a new romance of mine. I felt John was going to have quite an experience and I hoped he was up to that kind of catechism.

With a stab I realised that the chances were that he would say more to Percy, who was another man and a stranger, than he would to me, and that perhaps I would have to hear some of it secondhand. Yet I thought I could guess most of it.

At any rate, I got into my red wool and a coat faster than ever in my life, and was out on the road in less than five minutes.

I drove as if I was flying. The whole world seemed to have suddenly turned inside out and become marvellous. I know nothing of John's story except the one thing I suppose really mattered to me. He was in love with me still. I never doubted it. Whatever had happened was nothing to me. Whatever was coming to me, I did not care. Whatever the difficulties were, I felt certain we'd get over them. There was happiness ahead, real useful lives and happiness. It never occurred to me to remember I had something to forgive.

I was singing to myself, I think, as I drove down the lane. Certainly I waved at Miss Luftkin's house whether she was at the window to see me or not, and I pulled up outside Peacocks with a screech of brakes and a flurry of gravel.

Radek opened the door to me. His English was more than sketchy but he bowed to make up for it and said: 'Come, please,' and led me to the staircase.

I ran up it, I remember, striding across the landing behind him with an eagerness I had not known since my student days.

Grethe opened the bedroom door to me and I noticed that she was very pale. It was not so dark as on the night before. There was still some light from the windows and there was a lamp by the bed, but when Gastineau rose up from the shadows by the fireplace he took me by surprise. I had not expected him to be sitting there in the semi-darkness.

It was as I caught sight of him and was about to speak that I heard something from the bed that sent a chill through me. I turned away from him abruptly, so that he stood with hand still outstretched, and went over to it.

Francia Forde lay flat on her back, the light from the reading lamp full on her face.

She was breathing very slowly, with the deep stertorous respirations of coma, and her face was almost unrecognisable, it was so congested. I took her hand and it was flaccid and limp as a doll's.

No one came near me as I made my examination. I was quick but as thorough as I knew how to be, and every new discovery filled me with more and more alarm.

She had no reflexes. I could not believe it. I tested her again and again, motioning to Grethe to come closer and give me the help I needed. It was no good. I tried her eyes and found the pupils semi-dilated, which puzzled me. Her temperature was up a little, not very much.

My bewilderment increased. This was no logical continuation of the condition in which I had seen her eighteen or so hours before. My experience was not vast like Percy's but I was competent. I should never have made a mistake of that magnitude. At midnight this woman had been suffering from acute alcoholism, not very serious and one of the simplest things in the world to diagnose. Now she was in a deep coma which could have only one end, unless a miracle intervened.

I put some questions to Grethe, who answered them promptly, and my suspicions grew into terrifying certainty.

'How long has she been breathing like this?' I enquired.

The woman shrugged her shoulders and looked blank, so I put the vital enquiry into words.

'What has she taken during the day? What drug?'

This time Grethe decided not to understand me at all. She appealed to Gastineau and he came forward into the circle of light.

'This morning she was very excitable,' he began softly, 'almost demented. No one could do anything with her. Then at last she dropped into a sleep. At first no one worried but at four o'clock Grethe came up and was frightened, I think.'

She nodded vigorously and turned away. I didn't realise that she'd gone out of the room until I heard the door close softly.

'I shall need her,' I murmured. 'Will you call her back, please? I am afraid Madame Maurice is very ill.'

The news did not surprise him. His quiet dark eyes met mine.

'I will ring in a moment. Before that, though, there is something I think I should say to you, Doctor.' He looked towards the bed. 'You know who this is, don't you?'

I was silent a fraction too long and I heard him sigh.

'Of course you do. You recognised her last

70

night. Francia Forde, one of our leading film stars. A face that is very well known.'

He startled me horribly, not because he had told me anything new but because of a definite change in his attitude towards me. I took refuge in my most professional manner.

'I hardly think her identity is of any great importance just now,' I said briskly. 'What does matter is her condition. I tell you frankly that she has taken something since I saw her last, something—er—something of a strongly narcotic character, and if we are to save her life it is vital that I should know what it is. Do I make myself clear?'

I realised that things were going very wrong as I finished speaking. He showed no sign of any kind of feeling. He was not alarmed or worried or even particularly interested.

'You may be right,' he said gently. 'She was in a very strange mood when I persuaded her with such great difficulty to come with me into that ambulance which you so kindly arranged to send.'

I could hardly credit it, but there was, I was sure of it, a very definite emphasis on that last observation. It shook me. I certainly had hired the ambulance for him and because of one thing and another half the town was aware of the fact. However, there was nothing awkward in that unless . . . ?

The idea which had come into my head was so melodramatic that I discounted it at once.

71

People were kidnapped from time to time as I knew from the papers but when they were, surely they were never brought to ordinary places like Mapleford by ordinary people like Gastineau?

He had been watching me for some little time and presently he said something which set me back on my heels, while the hairs prickled on my scalp.

'I came to live in Mapleford solely because of you, Doctor. Did you know that?'

'No,' I declared, 'and I can't think—'

'Do forgive me for interrupting you.' His voice was gentle, even pleasant. 'I know how anxious you are to get on with your work. I just want to tell you that I felt sure you would recognise Francia Forde when you saw her, and I also felt that you would appreciate my introducing her here under a name that was not so well known as her own. There is some sort of etiquette in these matters, I think.'

'I had never seen Miss Forde before last night,' I began boldly.

'No.' He smiled at me as if he were explaining some small social matter. 'But you knew of her and you had good cause to—what shall we say—think of her quite a lot?'

There was a long silence. I think I was more terrified in that minute than ever before in my life.

He remained looking as I had always known him, bent and stiff and quietly polite.

'I think I am right when I guess that had you known who my Madame Maurice was you would have hesitated to associate yourself with any illness she might contract. You do realise how far you are committed, don't you, Dr. Fowler?'

Did I? Francia Forde was dying from a dose of poison, either self-administered or given her by this terrifying man in front of me. If there was ever any enquiry at all, it must emerge at once that it was I of all people who had cause not only to hate her but, since this afternoon, to be anxious to get her out of the way. As I cast around me, every circumstance in the past few days seemed to conspire to point at me.

I got a grip on myself. 'I think I must ask you to get other advice.' I heard the well-worn formula creep out in a little thin voice I scarcely knew. 'Since you're—you're so well informed, you'll understand that in the circumstances I really—really couldn't take the responsibility.'

'But of course you could and of course you will.' He spoke to me as if I were some kind of frightened child, scared of an exam. 'You'll do your utmost for my poor friend Madame Maurice, widow of an East European refugee. I fear it may be a long business. Pneumonia may intervene even, and if at last the worst should happen, then we know that a constitution weakened by alcoholism does often succumb to any acute pulmonary infection. Isn't that so?'

He was talking like a medical book, trying to put a formula into my mouth which could appear on a death certificate.

I gaped at him. Only the dreadful breathing from the bed convinced me that I was awake and facing reality.

It was an invitation to connive at murder. More than that, it was a threat, with my career and even my life as the alternative.

'This is nonsense,' I murmured. 'You're making an idiotic mistake. I must ask you to go to the telephone and call another doctor. Someone must treat this woman immediately, but it can't be me.'

'Don't you think so?'

As he spoke he stretched out his hand and slipped something into mine.

I looked down at it. It was the Dormital bottle and it was empty.

PART TWO

The great bedroom with its glistening black beam stretching across the low ceiling, and its diamond-paned windows letting in the last of the light, became very still.

The fire stirred and flared and a coal fell out onto the hearth with a ghost of a clatter. Peter Gastineau did not move. He stood a foot or so away from me, looking at me steadily with his expressionless eyes. Downstairs someone was rattling crockery and there was the sound of footsteps and a door closing.

I remained looking down at the little bottle in my hand. I had never thought so quickly or so clearly and it was natural that I should have done it in the way I had been taught.

In this predicament I was thinking medically, sorting out the things I knew for certain from the things that were as yet doubtful, and putting myself in the background and the life of the patient first. Now that I knew what the trouble was, and understood what had happened to the snoring bundle of humanity on the bed, every other consideration slid into second place. There had been fifty tablets in the bottle, each one five grains. I raised my eyes to Gastineau.

'Where did you get this?'

'From a shelf in the bathroom.' He pointed to a door which I had supposed to lead into a cupboard and turned back to meet my gaze impudently. 'I had never seen it before, of course.'

He was being the worried host again, completely acquiescent, leaving everything in my hands. Our conversation of a moment before might never have occurred.

As any doctor can explain, I ought at that moment to have fled. That move was the one thing that might have saved me. If I had done anything but stay—run to Percy, the police, anyone—I might just possibly have saved my own skin, but the woman would have died.

I didn't run. I thought she had an outside chance. People had survived larger doses.

As for the man in front of me, the fact that he was a potential murderer, that the Dormital was the Dormital I had lost, that he had trapped me deliberately, all these things still remained half proved. Had they been medical facts I should not have been justified in acting upon them from the evidence I had so far. I decided not to now. Besides, let me be honest, I was not afraid of Gastineau. I thought I knew him and could manage him. So I made up my mind and walked straight into nightmare.

'We must get a nurse at once,' I said.

He sighed. It was a little sound of pure relief. That ought to have settled it. It was my last chance, my last warning. I ignored it.

'Where is the telephone?'

'There is one in the hall and an extension in my sitting room. Is there anything I can do?'

'Yes, please. Get me Mapleford 234 and I'll follow you down.'

As soon as he was out of the room I went to the door and discovered, as I had hoped, that the key was still there. I took it and locked the patient in, and then I went downstairs. I suppose I thought it was going to be as easy as that.

The hall telephone was near the entrance and as soon as I came up Gastineau stepped back and handed me the receiver. He did not leave me, though. I could hear him breathing as he hovered in the background just out of my sight. The number I had given him was Nurse Tooley's and as I heard her voice my heart rose.

'It's Peacocks Hall, Nurse,' I began, speaking very quietly and hoping that she would use her wits. 'Could you come down at once and bring a night bag? I think you had better have your calls put through to Nurse Phillips. You may be out some time.'

'Something serious? I'll be there in a jiffy, Doctor.'

I blessed her calm acceptance of whatever was coming and trusted I wasn't dragging her into danger.

'Is there anything I can bring?'

'Well yes,' I said. 'Could you go round to the surgery and—Nurse?'

'I'm listening, Doctor.'

'Could you bring the—the *equipment* we

used on young George Roper some little time back? Do you remember?'

I heard her exclamation.

'The day he . . . ? Oh dear yes. You've got someone listening, I suppose? Do you expect trouble, Doctor?'

'I don't know,' I lied, 'but it's very urgent. If you'll go to the surgery and bring *everything* I'll get Mr. Gastineau to send his car down there for you.'

'I'll be there. Don't worry.'

'Bless you,' I said, and hung up. Then I put my head round the angle of the wall. 'Will you send the car, please?'

Gastineau was standing a few feet away, his hands in his pockets and his head bent. He glanced up sharply and there was a faint smile on his mouth.

'Do you really think it will do any good?'

It was that quiet man-to-man query, suggesting we were accomplices and emphasising the fact that we were alone, which gave me my first jolt after taking my decision to stay. I checked the retort which rose to my mouth and, feeling like a criminal, shrugged my shoulders.

'We must do everything we can.'

'But of course, Doctor.' He shot me an odd, half-admiring glance. 'I will call Radek. You shall give him the instructions yourself.'

There was nothing whatever I could do for the patient until Nurse arrived with her grisly

80

pumps and so I waited until I saw the man go and then I fetched my bag from the car and went upstairs again. There was no change and I expected none. Her heart was keeping up and I was certain I'd been right in deciding that there was no question of sending her to hospital. There were no pulmonary symptoms so far and I was not going to risk any by moving her an inch. Everything that was to be done, and there was plenty, would have to be performed right there in the room.

It had grown dark and I drew the curtains and turned up the lights, very glad of them somehow in that ancient shadowy bedchamber which must have seen generations of births and deaths in its four hundred years.

There was something which had to be done before Nurse arrived and I set about it. I went over the room like a police officer, searching it minutely for anything I could find. As I had expected, any suitcases which might have come with her had been removed. The drawers in the tallboy were completely empty. There was nothing in the wardrobe or on the chintz-skirted dressing table, not even a powder puff, a comb or a hairpin; nothing at all.

I investigated the bathroom and found that it literally was a cupboard, one of those enormous presses which are often built into the alcove of a fireplace in very old houses. It had been tiled in green and fitted up very cleverly with a tiny window high up over the

81

bath. There seemed scarcely room for anything to be hidden there, and yet I found something. Down on the floor; in the angle between the bath and the pedestal of the washbasin, was one of those flat plastic envelopes. It had not been noticed because it was the same colour as the tiles, and it was standing on its side flat against the wall and half hidden by a pastel-shaded towel. I pounced on it and pulled back the zipper. Inside there was a soggy mess of face towels, soap and odds and ends.

The first thing I pulled out was a nail brush, rather an elaborate affair, but sticky, of course, as everything else was. I turned it over with two fingers and stood looking at it. There was a monogram on the back, stamped into the ivory and picked out in green: F.F. Francia Forde.

So I was not dreaming and the thing was true. There was something about that utterly personal label which drove the facts home to me as nothing else would have done. Whatever the explanation of the whole crazy business might be, it truly was she and somehow or other I had got to save her life.

It was at that point that I heard someone try the door, and immediately afterwards a somewhat startled knocking. I thrust the brush back into the bag and dropped it where I had found it. If I had had the sense to go on examining it I might have been in a rather different frame of mind, but as it was I hurried out and opened the door to find a startled Nurse Tooley, with Radek, bundled up with gear, behind her.

I had seen Nurse Tooley arriving on a scene of trouble at least a dozen times in so many weeks, but as usual she gave me the small thrill of pure thankfulness. She kept Radek quiet and got the bags into the room without letting him enter. Her movements were light and neat and yet as powerful as a tractor. As she bent I saw her solidness and the width and power of her haunches under the stiff and pristine belt.

The moment the man had gone she closed the door very quietly and, with an eye on me, twisted the key softly in the lock. Then she pulled off her cloak, jerked the strings of her bonnet, and shot a long searching glance at the bed.

'Now, what have you got here?' she demanded.

I let her look and saw the deep frown appearing on her forehead. When she looked back at me I noticed with a pang that she was scared.

'What has she taken, by all the saints?'

'Some form of barbituric,' I said briefly, and it was the first time I had ever been evasive with Nurse Tooley.

'Indeed now.' She was startled and disapproving. 'I had in me mind something more homely, like the boy Roper you were mentioning.'

She was referring to a hectic afternoon we had spent together dealing with Mrs. Roper's youngest, who had eaten deadly nightshade berries and had worried us both stiff before we had got him through.

'I wish it were,' I said involuntarily. 'But the initial treatment's the same.'

'Ah, it would be,' she agreed with that heartening acquiescence I knew so well.

We got to work immediately. Nurse had obeyed me literally and had 'brought everything.' We did not have to appeal to anyone in the house. We had a fire and we had hot water; the rest she had brought with her.

I suppose it was nearly two hours before we said any word which was not purely to do with the job in hand. Long before then, whatever poison was left in the patient had been already absorbed. I completed the work and watched anxiously for any sign of improvement.

Francia lay flat on her back, her eyes closed, her breath still stertorous, and as I listened to her heart my own sickened. Despite the stimulants I had given, it was not quite so strong.

There was only one thing to do and that was to wait for a while. Nurse was clearing up at the far end of the room. I knew that at any moment now I must make her some sort of explanation and as I hesitated I saw out of the corner of my eye the Dormital bottle standing where I had left it on the corner of the chest nearest the bed.

There were one or two small ornaments on the glistening wood, a Spode bowl and a little lustre jug amongst them. I picked up the bottle and slid it into the jug for safety. It was practically a reflex action. I had no intention of doing anything secretive, but as Nurse turned round and caught me with my hand outstretched I coloured. There was nothing I could do to stop it.

She did not show any sign of noticing. Her own face was as placid and sensible as ever and she pulled a chair to the fire.

'Rest yourself, Doctor,' she suggested, her Irish voice soft and easy. 'It's terrible hard work you've been doing and there's nothing more to be done for her, poor soul, for a time at any rate.'

It was a straight invitation to talk, and I knew that with her I could take it or leave it as I chose. I went over and sat down and she eyed me with concern.

'You are tuckered up,' she observed. 'You're as white as linen. Wouldn't you like to run back for a minute or so, if it's only to have a bite of supper? I can well sit here, and if you think it's advisable to have the door locked, well, I can lock it.'

There was no query in her tone. I could explain just as much or as little as I liked and I knew then just why I had called her in and

85

nobody else. She was my insurance against any weakness which might lie within me. I knew that with her beside me I'd just have to do what was professional and correct, whatever the consequences. I respected her and I trusted her as I didn't seem to trust myself. She was a bridge I'd burned behind me.

'I don't want the patient left alone,' I said at last, 'unless the door is locked and the key is in your pocket or mine.'

This was a pretty startling statement and could only mean the obvious. She took it with a nod.

'Just as you say. There'll be no one comes anywhere near the poor little thing while I'm about.' She paused and added the one thing which could have shown me just how completely in the picture she was. 'There'll be no windows left open by mistake to give her pneumonia while I'm around.' And she leant forward to make up the fire, the red glow shining on the white linen of her cap. 'Well now, why don't you treat yourself to half an hour at home?'

I shook my head. John was at the cottage and frankly I did not dare to think about him. His appearance had made the present situation so appallingly dangerous that I felt that the only thing to do was to keep him out of my mind and trust to God that he would not enter into anybody else's. I relied on Rhoda to explain where I was. His own intelligence would tell him that something fairly serious was amiss, and I trusted he'd do the sane thing and get quietly back to Grundesberg. Personal matters were not thinkable at that moment, and the new warmth which suffused me and was making me so reckless gave me a guilty feeling I certainly wasn't going to analyse.

Nurse Tooley folded her hands in her starched lap and raised her neat head.

'Would this be the young party that was brought down from London in the ambulance there was all the talk about?'

I felt my heart miss a beat. 'Talk?'

She smiled at me apologetically. 'There's one thing I don't believe in and that's gossip,' she murmured. 'It's an evil in this town, God knows. But you know there was a bother about the whole business, don't you?'

'I knew the time was changed at the last moment,' I said cautiously.

'Ah, that put them out to begin with, no doubt, but they had trouble at the house, you know. There was no one there but a woman no one took a fancy to, and the patient was in a highly peculiar state.'

She cast her eyes down and let me think what I would.

'There was no one who could do anything with her except this Mr. Gastineau, who had come with them, and there was a misunderstanding about yourself not being there to meet them.'

87

In her attempt to let me down lightly she succeeded in painting a scarifying picture, and I could just imagine how the tale would run round Mapleford.

Her pretty voice continued softly.

'But it's all completely all right because everyone knew it was you, Doctor, who was arranging the matter.'

I was trying to decide what would be the most sensible comment to make when she forestalled me.

'But early this morning when the stranger came round asking questions, everyone was interested, naturally.'

I don't think I could have moved had I dared. I had heard of people feeling that their blood had turned to ice water and for the first time I could believe it.

'What stranger was this?' I hoped my voice sounded more normal to her than it did to me.

'From what Mr. Robins the Superintendent said, he was very pleasant but kind of simple.' She made the words sound kindly and I suddenly knew who she meant although there was no reason why I should have guessed it.

'Was he carrying an umbrella?' The words were nearly out of my mouth but I checked them. The man had succeeded in rattling me in London, but never so much as now.

Nurse Tooley was laughing. 'Mr. Robins took pity on him and told him where to get rooms, poor soul. He seemed to have just stepped off the train without making any arrangements. What people will do!'

I got up. That final exclamation of hers had come straight home. What people will do! I knew what *I had* to do. The decision had arrived ready-made in my mind some few minutes before. The time had come.

I gave Nurse the necessary instructions with regard to the patient and told her to call me the moment she thought she noticed any change, and then I let myself out into the dark upper hall and went downstairs. The old house was very quiet and oddly serene. Its very naturalness made the horror around me seem worse and more peculiarly my own. It was as though I had brought it there. I knew my way about, of course, and making as little noise as possible, I walked into the sitting room and across it before Gastineau was aware.

He was sitting in his chair by the fire and the room looked just as it always did, very comfortable and civilised. The desk was just as untidy as when I'd seen it last and the little drawer which Gastineau had closed so quickly was still shut. It looked as though nothing had been touched.

I walked straight over to it, ignoring him, and pulled it open. There were all kinds of rubbish there, string, paper clips, a roll of tape, but no blue pamphlet.

The man behind me did not move. His eyes had been on me ever since I entered but he

89

had not stirred. His stiff legs were turned to the blaze and his hands remained in his lap. As I shut the drawer he smiled at me.

'You did notice? I wondered, but I wasn't sure. It was a bad moment for me. I thought I would be on the safe side.' He nodded at the fire pointedly.

I pulled up a chair opposite him and sat down, and as I did so I caught a glimpse of myself in a long narrow mirror on the further wall. It startled me. I looked much younger, much more feminine and less impressive than I had thought. I wondered if he really did see me as just a pretty girl. If so, it was an image that had got to be dispelled.

'Look here,' I announced as unequivocally as I knew how, 'I want an explanation.'

His eyes met mine and I was aware of a sort of quietude, a contentment which I had not seen there before.

'But of course you do,' he agreed. 'How understandable that is. But you know I don't think it is wise.'

It was the last attitude I had expected him to take. I had to struggle to keep the initiative.

'That's for me to decide.'

'Perhaps so.' He offered me a cigarette box from the telephone table at his elbow, and when I refused took one himself.

'What do you want to know?' He was pleasant and conversational. We might have been talking of anything in the world.

'When did Madame—Miss Forde go to Barton Square?'

'A little over a week ago.'

'Why did she go there?' If he preferred to do it this way I did not mind. I was not moving unless Nurse called me.

'I took her there,' he said at last. 'We had been dining together.'

'And left her there?'

'Yes.' He laughed at my expression and I had to take a grip on myself. I had known patients who had played the fool like this when they were monkeying with the truth.

'Explain,' I snapped.

He hesitated for a long time and finally shrugged.

'You are a good doctor, I think. You probably saw for yourself that she had recently taken—what shall we call it, a little sedative.'

'In fact you drugged her.'

He spread out his hands. 'Well, that is a theatrical way of putting it. I gave her an opiate. It is a prescription I have had for many years and have used myself when I had much pain. When she became sleepy I took her to Barton Square, where I had a very good friend who looked after her . . .'

'And kept her prisoner?' I demanded, aghast.

'Not at all. She was persuaded to stay.' He spoke easily and rationally, and it occurred to me that he had had experience of being

91

questioned. There was something skilled in his little retreats and omissions. 'She waited until I could make arrangements and come to fetch her.'

'Do her friends know where she is now?'

For the first time I saw him waver. 'Perhaps not,' he said at last. 'You see, Doctor, there is a little secret about Francia. It is the thing which tempted me to—well, to persuade her to come here in the way I did persuade her. Just before her last film was made she had some sort of *crise de nerfs* and it was discovered, with dismay, that she had taken refuge in alcohol. It was all kept very dark, you understand. An eminent specialist prescribed. She went into a nursing home and she was cured. Splendid. The incident was forgotten. The new film was made. Everyone was delighted. And then this magnificent offer from Moonlight came along, and she was photographed from morning to night, very successfully, I believe.'

He paused, and I saw something so cold and so terrible in his face that I had to master an actual fear of him.

'I have kept a very careful eye on her for some time and I was one of the few who knew about that breakdown,' he went on at last, adding calmly, 'It occurred to me that such a thing could so easily happen again . . .'

'That's abominable!' I exploded, and he watched me placidly.

'Do you think so? It was not very difficult to

arrange at Barton Square, I assure you. She was angry and alarmed and the alcohol was there. I did it because it was so convenient. You see, I felt certain that when she vanished those nearest to her would jump at once to a certain conclusion and would probably keep quiet. On the other hand, if they did not, and by some bad luck she was found before I was ready, well, it would appear to be just as they had feared.'

The sheer wickedness of it appalled me. I leaned forward.

'And you brought her here in an ambulance because you knew no one would query it, getting a doctor to order it for you to make yourself doubly safe?'

'No.' For the first time he came back at me and his dull eyes became bright and alive. 'You are forgetting. I got not *a* but *the* doctor to order it for me, and to go to Barton Square where she was noticed. I should not be surprised if you called considerable attention to yourself when you saw no ambulance there. Did you ask a policeman?'

I didn't answer that. 'A doctor or the doctor, it makes no difference.'

'But it does.' The gentle voice was soothing and it filled me with sheer terror. 'Of course it does. Come, you are a realist, you are not a fool. We have discussed this already. You know where you stand.'

He was getting the upper hand. It was

becoming his interview. I sidetracked to get it back again.

'Who was the deaf woman I saw at Barton Square?'

'The Ukrainian servant of my friend. She would have been alone in the house when you arrived.'

'And who was the man with the umbrella?'

Gastineau was puzzled by that. I could see it in his face.

'Where did you find him? In the kitchen?'

'Yes. What's more, I think he's followed us down here. He's been asking questions at the ambulance station.'

This information did not alarm him in the least. He swept the news away with a flicker of a finger.

'It may be someone who is employed by my friend in Barton Square. Women are inquisitive and sometimes jealous. There is nothing in that.'

To my horror, I discovered that I was finding him reassuring.

'What was your reason?' I demanded suddenly. It was the shock of mistrusting myself which made the question come out so brashly. All the time I had been wondering about it, but to ask it outright meant that I accepted—well, the thing I wasn't accepting.

He understood me at once. It was still the most frightening thing about him that we did understand each other so well, as I had noticed long before. He looked down at his knees, the wooden stiffness of his legs, and peered up at me from under his lids without moving his bent back.

'I was a tall man at one time,' he remarked unexpectedly and with a detachment which I found unnerving. 'I walked a great deal. Mountain climbing was my hobby. I was also very sensitive to my surroundings. Sordidness, ugliness, anything dirty or cruel disgusted me physically.' He stopped, his flat eyes still watching me. 'If you want to know you must listen to this. It won't take very long.'

'Go on,' I said.

"There was a time in my life,' he continued quietly, 'when I was in business in Stockholm. It was just before the war. During that time I was able to do certain little services for my own country. I shall not explain them but you must understand that they were secret. And, since I was able to enter into the high circles in Germany and Austria, of some little use. Do you understand?'

'You were a spy,' I suggested bluntly.

'No. If that were true I should be dead by now. No, I was in effect a confidential messenger, no more.'

'I see.'

He nodded and continued. 'I was in love with a woman who was very much younger than I. She had come to the country with a dancing troupe which had been stranded, leaving her with a British passport and not much else. When I first saw her it was in the summer and she was trying to persuade a business friend of mine to give her a job dancing and singing in his restaurant. She had no voice and her shabby little clothes hung on her like paper streamers on one of those wands you buy on a fairground.'

There was no actual change in his tone, which was still quietly conversational, but there was a force there which I recognised. It was an emotional thing. I knew it only too well.

'I was not very rich,' he said slowly, 'but I was not poor, and there was something indefinable about her which attracted me. I got her her job and I saw that she had something to wear. She accepted anything I offered eagerly, her passion to get on somehow at all costs amused me. I saw a great deal of her after that and gradually a terrible thing happened to me and I fell in love with her.'

He was still watching me. 'Not everybody loves,' he observed at last. 'With some people it is a ghost of a thing, a flare in the night which is bright and transfiguring and then . . . gone. But with others, and I think you know all about this, it is a most dreadful power, frightening and devouring and inescapable.'

I tried to shut him out of my sympathies.

'I just want the facts,' I murmured as if he were describing a set of symptoms.

'But that is *the* fact,' he protested. 'You know that as well as I do. I loved this girl in that particular way, and because she was the kind of woman she is I was soon near ruin and I had to tell her so. I do not think I have ever horrified anyone more, even you, dear Doctor.' He laughed a little, but not with amusement. 'Fortunately, I still had the little money on which I now live tied up in England, but by then the war had begun. The time came when I had to make one of my regular journeys to Berlin. Because I was in love with her I trusted her with a secret connected with my trip. It was only a little thing, mercifully—I carried no papers. It was no more than that I had to go to a certain man and tell him that the answer was yes. In my complete infatuation, perhaps because I was insane enough to imagine it might make her think more of me, I let her know I was not going solely on business.'

I knew what was coming. It was clear in his dark ugly face. There was nothing to guess, even.

'Yes,' he agreed, as if I had spoken, 'she sold the information. I was of no further use to her so she took the last there was to be got out of me. She whispered the news at a party where she was dancing, wearing a dress I had chosen for her and jewels I had given her. The man she told paid her in cash. And as for me, when I reached the little house in the German capital, I was arrested. The rest I will not speak about!'

The last words came out with passion and brought me half to my feet. I hardly recognised him in the blazing, bitter wreck before me. He thrust out his hands, which were already malformed, and his gesture embraced the rest of his warped and tortured body.

'You *know*,' he said. 'There is no more for me to tell you about that. You are a doctor. You can comprehend something of that imprisonment.'

I said the one thing that I could say to that. 'Are you sure?'

'Sure it was she? Sure it was done for money and to get rid of me? Yes.' It was final, a very softly spoken word.

I have said somewhere that I myself am frightened of hatred and that I have always fled from it lest it should consume me. As I looked at him I knew what had happened to him as surely as if he had shown me a gangrenous joint. He *was* the ash of hatred. It had got him and poisoned him and made him mad.

He went on talking quietly again now and almost pleasantly.

'I could not face discomfort and hideousness again. I could not risk any kind of imprisonment, anything ugly or terrible. I had to find a way to punish her that for me was quite safe. I had to have help. So when that

98

other woman in Barton Square, who has always watched my affairs so carefully, showed me a cutting from a magazine which she had saved, and I found out that there was another person who had cause to hate Francia as much as I did . . .'

'No.' The word was jerked out of me and it sounded frightened. He went on as if I had not spoken.

'When I discovered that not only did such a person exist, but that she was a doctor, someone in the ideal position to make what I had to do perfectly simple and perfectly safe, then I felt that there was justice in the world, and I came here to Mapleford to find you.'

'Yes,' I said cautiously, feeling my way as one does when the disease is new to one and shocking. 'But when you saw me didn't you realise that it wouldn't work?'

'When I saw you,' he said contentedly, 'I recognised you, or rather I recognised something in you. You were drowning yourself in work, hiding in it, but you were not quite escaping, were you? I saw that if I put the idea to you you would do your best to have me certified insane, but I guessed that if the *fait accompli* were presented to you suddenly I should get my way and you would help me.' He threw the butt of his cigarette into the fire. 'And I was right,' he said.

'No.' I spoke as quietly as he had done. He had ceased to terrify me. I had begun to see

99

him as a pathetic pathological case with which in other circumstances I could even have sympathised. 'You're making a mistake.'

'I don't think so. You have imagination. You know what will happen to you if you do not do your part. There are too many coincidences for you to explain in any police enquiry. Besides, this is the woman who stole your name. Since then you have not even considered anyone else. Your neighbours have noticed it. "The little doctor has taken a knock. She hasn't forgotten it." Isn't that what they say?'

I ignored the last part of that and tried to reason with him. He was sane enough in every particular save one.

'Don't you see,' I said gently, 'all this happened some years ago? If I was upset then, I did nothing about it. Why should anyone believe that I should seek out Francia Forde now?'

I saw the doubt creeping over him. His own hatred had been kept alive so long by his sufferings. He had identified mine with it.

'But you stayed tonight.'

'I hope to save her.'

'You won't.' It was as though he knew something I didn't. For a second he had me off balance. 'You knew it tonight,' he said. 'That was why you sent for the nurse you felt you could trust. I could tell from the way you spoke to her you were certain she would never give you away. Perhaps she is too stupid or perhaps she is too dependent on you. It is one or the other.'

'You're wrong.' Now it was my words which were really convincing. There was triumph in them; I couldn't keep it out. 'I chose Nurse Tooley because I trust her more than I do myself. She's my sheet anchor.' That was the first time I frightened him. He understood exactly what I meant, as I had known he would.

'You wouldn't have dared.' He was appealing, he was hoping, not accusing, and he went on talking still with the trace of uncertainty. 'It was the only thing which made me wait so long. You give this profession of yours the passion you ought to give a lover. It is a religion with you. Yet you'll ruin your career if you don't go through with this.'

'Should the patient die I shall have to risk that.' I believed it and I said it and it sounded true.

He lay back in the chair and stared at me. There was astonishment there, that and chagrin.

I don't know what would have happened then. There's a chance he would have cracked, or he might have gone for me, I don't know . . . At that precise instant something happened which defeated me. It was the unkindest trick pure chance ever played. The telephone bell began to ring.

Gastineau was between me and the instrument and he took up the receiver.

'Yes. Yes, I will tell her, she is here. Who shall I say is calling?'

I was watching him and I saw the change in his face. The blood raced into its greyness and his eyes grew bright. He turned to me with a smile of victory.

'It is for you. Dr. John Linnett.'

It was nearly half a minute before I took the receiver. My first impulse had been not to take it at all. When I did, my hand shook and I held my elbow to keep it still.

John's voice came through strong and natural and faintly apologetic.

'Ann, this is to warn you. I'm running down to say good night.'

I moved back as far as I could from the man in the chair. The cord was very short.

'Oh no,' I said firmly, 'no, I shouldn't do that.'

'Why not?' I knew that tone of John's. I had heard it a thousand times, from nursery days on. It meant he was going to have his own way. 'I shan't keep you a minute,' he said. 'I'll be at the front door in something under a quarter of an hour. I shall ring the bell like a proper little practitioner and ask for you, and you're to come out. Do you hear? Got that? Just say "yes," and tell whoever's listening it's the Ministry of Health.'

'No,' I said again but he rang off.

102

I looked up at last to find Gastineau considering me speculatively. I said nothing. There was nothing I could say, and presently I turned and went out of the room. As I reached the doorway he spoke.

'At any rate we know each other a little better, Doctor.'

I left him sitting there and went up the stairs again and across the deserted upper hall. From the grandfather in the corner I saw that I had not been away more than twenty minutes. I could have believed it twenty years.

Nurse Tooley had got the door locked and she arrived in something of a flutter in answer to my tap.

'Oh, it's you, praise be,' she murmured. 'I was wondering if I'd call you.'

I looked at the bed eagerly but she shook her head. 'No change at all, poor soul, no change at all. The heart's keeping up, though.'

'Thank God,' I said fervently. There was not a lot more I could do. While her heart remained strong and there was no sign of lung trouble it was best to let the body do what it could for itself.

Nurse Tooley kept her bright eyes on my face. She was more flushed than usual and there was a hint of defiance in her which was new to me.

'Will you look here, Doctor?' She pointed to something on the dressing table and we went over towards it together. It was the green plastic envelope which I had found in the bathroom and had not had time to examine properly. Nurse had been more thorough. The entire contents was laid out neatly on a folded towel, ready for me to see.

'It's the only thing in the world the poor thing has with her,' she confided to me in a whisper, 'or so you'd imagine from the nakedness of this room.'

I glanced at the exhibits and looked again. The usual paraphernalia was all there, but there was something else, something new which I had not found in my interrupted search. It was a little heap of small white pills and the sodden screw of paper which had once contained them. There were twenty-two of them, battered and sticky but still recognisable. I could make out a roman numeral stamped on the surface of the one I picked up.

I could guess what it was before I touched it with my tongue and tasted the bitterness.

'What is it, Doctor? Luminal?'

'I don't know.' I spoke woodenly because my heart had sunk with a thud. This explained the mystery of the deep and prolonged coma, which had been puzzling me. It also explained Gastineau's belief that Francia would die. 'It's one of them.'

'It's one of them.' Nurse's conviction echoed my own. 'Medinal, Dial . . . something. You see, she's been in the habit . . .'

I cut her short. She had gone straight to the point, as usual. That was what this discovery meant, Francia Forde was in the habit of taking barbituric acid in some form, and one of its peculiarities is that it is cumulative. It remains in the system a considerable time. Therefore the sudden dose of Dormital must have merely added to the sum already in her body. There was no knowing what the total might be.

That it was a habit was clear The patient who is given a few grains by his doctor to take in case of insomnia hardly keeps them loose in a sponge bag. This contempt indicated a very considerable familiarity. I supposed she had been given them after her 'breakdown.'

While I was digesting this appalling consideration Nurse Tooley made a remark which took some seconds to register on me.

'Well, at any rate we know what it is. That's a tremendous comfort if anything should happen to the poor thing.'

It was the way she said it which startled me. There was a note in her voice which I had never heard there before. It matched the hint of defiance I had noticed in her manner. At last I recognised it. She was guilty about something.

My eyes strayed across the room, past the vast bed with its tragic little burden, and over to the chest. The lustre jug had been moved several inches nearer to the wall. I turned to

Nurse and looked at her. She became very red and the involuntary thought shot through my mind that any prosecuting lawyer would have the time of his life with her if ever he got her on the stand. She was not designed for subterfuge.

When I went to the chest and looked the jug was empty.

'Nurse.'

Her back was to me. She was poking the fire and making a blaze. The flame and her face were just about the same colour. She took a minute to make up her mind and then straightened her back, the iron poker still in her hand, so that she looked like something allegorical in a village pageant.

'I soaked off the label and put it in the fire, and I smashed up the bottle on the hearth and put the pieces down the drain. So now you know.'

I couldn't believe it. The statement took all the breath out of my body. I must have goggled at her. She came a step or two forward, still grasping the poker.

'Now, look, Doctor dear'—her accent had become as broad as her beam—'I'm an old woman by the side of yourself and I'm imploring you. There's never one word will be passed between the two of us or any other living soul on the subject again. There's no one knows better than I do what people will do. They'll pick up something out of your bag and leave it lying around for the first poor crazy thing that comes to the house to pick up.'

She was so earnest that her kind eyes were full of tears and she trembled till her apron crackled.

'I know. I've seen even more than you have. But you're a fine doctor, conscientious, and as brave as a lion, and I'm not going to see you held up while the Coroner makes damaging remarks on carelessness and suchlike rubbish. As soon as I saw those little pellets in her sponge bag I said to myself, "Here's something that will do, sent by the Lord."'

Had I heard it at any moment but that one I could have laughed. As it was, I nearly wept. This was the first thing that she or I had done in the whole business which was actually wrong. We might have been silly but we hadn't been criminal. Without this I could have told my story and stuck to it and held my head up and prayed that the truth would save me. But this complicated the issue. This destroying the bottle proved that at any rate we weren't half-witted and that we knew what was happening.

'Holy Mother, have I made a fool of meself?'

'No,' I said hastily, trying to forget that I'd been relying on her for moral support, 'No, it'll be all right . . .' and got no further because a tap on the door interrupted me. Nurse went over and came back with a note.

'The foreign manservant's waiting outside

for an answer,' she murmured.

The letter was from Miss Luffkin and it was typical.

My dear Doctor,

Very worried indeed to gather someone so ill. What can I do? Do not hesitate to ask anything. Would milk pudding help? Have some real rice, sent in parcel nephew America. Have telephoned Dr. Ludlow, since did not care to interrupt your work. He says not to worry as you are very capable. Know that, of course, but feel you are so slight and young. Forgive me, I see you have that good nurse with you so suppose you can manage, but perhaps Dr. Ludlow will run down. Always remember I am here.

Ever yours sincerely,
Gertrude Elizabeth Luffkin

P.S. Have spoken on phone to Miss Farquharson, Mrs. Dorroway and Betty Phelps in the village. They all say you must let them know if there is anything they can do to help. Shall run down with this myself.

It was the final line which I found most alarming and I went to the door to speak to Radek. He seemed to share my anxiety, for he pointed to the floor below and put a thick finger over his lips. I took his tip and pencilled,

'Nothing now, but thank you. Please don't worry, but get some sleep. A.F.' on the back of the envelope, and sent him down with it. I felt safer when the door was locked again.

I went back to the bed. Percy might turn up if she had been worrying him. It would hasten matters if he did. I had made up my mind to be quite frank with him and to take what was coming.

I went over the patient again. The breathing had not changed, the pulse was faint, and the temperature had risen half a degree. She was bathed in perspiration. The lungs were still all right.

'What a pretty woman,' said Nurse, her homely face full of pity. 'She's put me in mind of someone I've seen somewhere. Maybe one of the Holy Angels in the pictures. It would be that fair hair, no doubt. Do you know who she is at all?'

'Yes,' I said. 'Her name is Forde.'

It meant nothing to Nurse but it carried full weight with me. Until then I had striven to achieve the impersonal attitude which a doctor must preserve if he is to do any good and yet not tear himself to a rag. The chance remark had broken it down and from that moment on her identity was as vivid to me as if I had been confronted with her alive and well. I could see her walking on those long slender legs, turning that perfectly shaped yellow head and smiling, perhaps.

I checked myself. This was not the time to bear even the recollection of jealousy. The new information made things just as bad as they could be. I began to see just exactly what was most likely to happen. The probability was that in the next twenty-four hours the coma would become even deeper and the heart, despite my stimulants, would slowly, slowly fail. Then, in the dawn perhaps, defeating all our efforts while Nurse and I looked at her, both of us impotent and exhausted, it would flutter and be still. We should try artificial respiration. We should try everything. We should wear ourselves to shreds. But it would be as hopeless as I ought to have known it would be, and I should do what I had to do and tell the police.

I had no illusions. I could see the rags of my career fluttering down over me like dead leaves. If that was all I should be lucky. If Gastineau stuck to the story he was clearly intending to tell I should find myself on a criminal charge, *for this was Francia.* I hated her. I still hated her, God forgive me. Somehow or other I had got to save her life and have her still tied to John. Otherwise very probably I should find myself arrested for murder.

I was not going to be able to save her. That conviction crept into my consciousness like a very small thin knife entering a vital part. There is no other way of describing it. It gave me that physical sense of extreme danger and despair which is like nothing else.

'Look out!' It was Nurse. She came round the bend and caught my arm. 'You've overdone it, Doctor me dear. I don't want you on my hands as well. Put your head down. Wait, I'll get a chair and have you round in a jiffy.'

I drew away from her and attempted a laugh. 'I'm all right,' I said, 'honestly. Look. Perfectly steady now. It was a little hot in here.'

'I believe you're right.' Her relief was tremendous. 'You gave me quite a turn for a moment. Upon me soul, every shred of colour went out of your face. You looked like a corpse. I'll get meself down to the kitchen and see if anyone in this benighted house can make a Christian cup of coffee.'

It seemed a most sensible suggestion and I returned to the bed as she went out. But she was back in a moment, very startled and put out.

'It's himself, the foreigner, standing on the landing. He wants a word with you in private,' she whispered. 'He said he'd not got as far as knocking and I think it's true.'

'I'll go,' I murmured. 'Stay with the patient.'

Gastineau was waiting for me and it was evident that something had happened. He was angry and his stiff hands were trembling.

'What have you done?' he demanded. 'The

111

police have been on the telephone.'

'The police?' I had not known I could start so guiltily. 'What about?'

'That is what I want to know. I told them you were busy with your patient, who was very ill, and they asked would you ring back.'

I glanced at the clock. It was nearly ten, late for ordinary business calls from the police or anyone else. Gastineau was eyeing me suspiciously.

'Have you no idea at all?'

'None.'

'Have you communicated with them in any way?'

'No.'

His catechism had the merciful effect of annoying me and restoring my wits.

'I can't imagine what they want,' I said briskly. 'We'd better go and see. You can listen to the conversation if you want to.'

He gave me the half-admiring glance I had seen from him once or twice before and came awkwardly down the steps behind me. His experiences had crocked him very badly, I reflected. He must have been continually in pain.

I made for the telephone and had almost reached it when Radek came hurrying past me from the kitchen to answer the front doorbell. As he swung the wood open I looked up and all thought of the phone or the police went out of my head in a wave of dismay. John was standing on the step, his coat collar turned up and his shoulders dark with rain. He saw me at once and did not smile.

'Oh, there you are, Dr. Fowler,' he began with becoming formality. 'Can I speak to you for a moment, please? I have a message for you. It's rather urgent. Will you come out to the car?'

I was prepared for Gastineau to protest and braced myself to avoid an introduction at all costs, but when he made no movement forward but limped back to the living room I knew that the thing I dreaded most of all had happened. He had recognized either John's voice from the telephone, or face from a photograph, and so from henceforth John was implicated however much I tried to save him.

Meanwhile, John had stepped into the house and put the rug he had brought round my shoulders. He said nothing but bundled me off and I was outside and into the car before I could protest. He shut me in and went round to the driving seat, opened the door, and glanced not at me but at the dark well behind me.

'Well, this is the place,' he said cheerfully to someone in the blackness. 'If you want Peacocks Hall this is it.'

I dragged away the shrouding rug which had all but blinded me just in time to see a tall, apologetic figure climbing out.

'How stupid of me. Thank you very much,

113

sir, thank you. Dear me, I had no idea we had arrived.'

I recognised that misleadingly helpless voice on the first syllable.

'Very good of you,' it was saying. 'I shall go round to the back door, I think. Thank you so much. Good-bye.'

He looked back, saw me, and raised his hat politely in recognition before he disappeared in the downpour, still clutching his unopened umbrella.

I think that was the final shock which broke me. I heard myself babbling, apparently from a long way off.

'Oh, why did you bring him here? Why? Who is he? Who is he?'

'Here . . . hey, old lady, what's up'

A very strong damp arm took a grip round my shoulders.

'What's the matter?'

'Where did you find him?' I was gibbering, powerless to control myself.

'That old boy? On the road, just outside your cottage. He hailed me and asked me if I knew of a place called Peacocks. I told him to get in and I'd take him there. I shoved him in the back because he was so wet and I wanted to keep this pew dry for you.'

This reasonable explanation all but paralysed me.

'But that's the man who was at Barton Square,' I chattered. 'That's the man who followed . . .'

'Stop it.' The flat of his hand caught me sharply across the wrist and the stinging pain brought me to myself. I heard my sob of relief as I regained balance. The time-honoured cure for hysteria had saved another patient.

John's grip round me tightened and he pulled me to face him in the faint glimmer from the dashlight. The familiar bones of his face and the tones of his voice were sources of actual physical strength to me. I felt, absurdly, that I was home again.

'Listen, Annie.' It was the name he gave me to tease me when I was in disgrace with him in the schoolroom. 'I've had a chat with Rhoda and I know who your patient is. Tell me, *what is she up to?*'

'It's not that.' I had got myself in hand again. 'You must go at once, John. Get back to Grundesberg and don't tell a soul where you've been.'

'Damn good idea,' he agreed 'We'll both go.'

'No. This is serious, John. She's going to die.'

'Francis?' He whistled softly. 'Oh, I see what you mean.' There was no deep concern there. To my disgust I found I'd listened for it. 'What's the trouble?'

'An overdose of barbituric acid, various forms.'

I felt him go stiff at my side.

'Hell!'

'Exactly.' I spoke very softly and urgently. 'That's why you've got to vanish. It's for my sake quite as much as your own. You do see, don't you?'

'Coroner's inquest and stink generally. And me calling on you? Oh, Lord, what have I let you in for? Yes, you're right, Ann. The only thing I can do is to beat it.'

I think it was my very silence which gave me away. I was so anxious for him to escape it all I could hardly breathe. He guessed. He knew me too well. His grip grew tighter.

'Ann, speak up. Why did she take the stuff?'

I didn't lie to him. I couldn't. Besides, he'd have to know sooner or later. I moistened my lips.

'She didn't take it. She had it given her.'

The words sank into the silence and their tiny echo hung in the darkness for a long time. John moved. It was typical of him, as I remembered, that in the face of real trouble he should become quiet and gently matter-of-fact. He removed his arm from my shoulder and laid his hand over mine.

'Just give the facts,' he said softly. 'The whole thing. Start at the beginning. Don't try to go too fast'

I gave up trying to resist. It was like telling myself. I went through the whole thing, keeping my voice normal, even conversational. It was just one doctor telling another about a

116

case.

I hid nothing. I let every damning circumstance have its full value—the Dormital, Nurse's destruction of the bottle, the ordering of the ambulance, the visit to Barton Square, and the man I'd seen there.

He listened to me in silence to the end. Then he bent down and kissed the top of my head very lightly.

'Added to which, you and I were discovered by old Dr. Consequential lying in each other's arms this very afternoon.' He made the statement with finality and opened the door of the car.

'What are you doing?' I demanded.

'Coming in.' He leaned over the seat and hauled a battered leather bag out of the back. 'I've seen a couple or so of these cases. I'd better stay.'

'That,' said I, coming out of a trance, 'is pure madness. You can't attend your own wife, John. You're jeopardising everything.'

'My dear girl,' he objected, 'everything is jeopardised, as you call it. You and I might as well be in the dock this minute.'

'I might,' I agreed. 'I've realised that for the last half hour. But not you. You can prove you'd not heard from me since 1945, until you got Rhoda's telegram yesterday.'

He made no reply to that but continued his manoeuvres.

'Come on,' he said.

'I won't let you do this,' I said. I was obstinate. 'I refuse to allow it. I won't let you into this case and ruin yourself for my sake.'

He came round to open my door for me and bent to help me out. His face was expressionless.

'Then perhaps you'll let me do it for hers,' he said distinctly.

It was the same technique as the slap, but applied emotionally. Even though I recognised it, it had its effect. It reminded me exactly where I stood. A man had jilted me and made a fool of me, and four years later he had walked into my house and held out his arms. Without the faintest hesitation I had pitched myself neatly into them. It wouldn't be difficult for me to discover that I'd got exactly what I deserved for that. It broke down my resistance very effectively.

'I must phone the police as soon as I get in,' I said. 'I told you.'

'Yes. Any idea what that's about?'

'No. Unless this man you brought here is anything to—to do with them.'

John considered. 'I rather think not. Better get in and find out.'

We went quietly back to the house. There was no one in the hall and as he slipped off his wet things I got on the phone. I was answered at once by Sergeant Archer and he appeared to have been waiting for me. I recognised that catarrhal voice and was reminded painfully of

118

our last encounter at the road accident, when I had been so abrupt with him.

' 'Ullo, Doctor, that you? Mapleford Division of the County Constabulary 'ere. It's a little matter of a dangerous drug.'

'Yes,' I said faintly.

'Dormital. I'll spell it, if I may.' The thick voice was heavily official. 'D, Ho, R, M, I, T, A, L. One two-ounce bottle containing fifty five-grain tablets or cachets. Is that right?'

'Tablets, not cachets.'

'Tab-lets.' He was writing, taking his time. 'Thank you, Doctor. Reported lost at 3:00 P.M, on the 12th inst. Sorry to bother you when you're busy, but records are records and have to be kept. Now it 'as come to our knowledge in a highly irregular way that there is every likeli'ood of you 'aving found these 'ere tablets by this time—'

'What?' I felt my scalp prickling.

'Pardon, Doctor.' He was heavily polite. 'Dr. Ludlow was having a chat with our Inspector Brush and it was said . . .'

I breathed a little more easily. I saw what had happened. Percy had told Brush not to worry and Brush had told Archer not to worry, but Archer had seen a chance of getting his own back on me on the pretence of getting his records straight. I did not even hear the end of the sentence. What I did hear was his next question. It came clearly across the line.

'Have you in fact found these tablets,

119

Doctor?'

Don't lie. Whatever you do, don't lie. Every instinct I possessed seemed to be screaming at me. I could have screamed myself, I think, but presently I heard my own voice, very crisp and formal.

'Yes, I have. A few hours ago. Since then I have been very busy, as I am at this moment. I will make my report in writing tomorrow morning. Good-bye.'

I hung up and walked out into the hall. I felt as if the rope were already round my neck.

John was waiting for me, his dark red eyebrows raised. I gave him a murmured explanation and he frowned.

'Awkward. Still, the only thing you could have done in the circumstances. Lord, what a mess! Why is your old boss so anxious to keep quiet about the stuff?'

'He has a horror of scandal.' I was looking at his face and I saw his wide mouth twitch and the flicker in his eyes. It was the most characteristic grin in the world, expressing pure humour, sardonic and his own. It brought the reality of his return home to me more vividly than anything else had done.

'Unlucky man,' he murmured. 'Now, where is your avenging lunatic?'

I pointed to the living-room door. 'And the kitchen quarters are down there at the back,' I said. 'That man who came with you . . .'

He shook his head. 'None of that is our

affair. We're doctors, not policemen. Where's the patient?'

He was right, of course. I felt rebuked for even thinking of anything else and I led him up the staircase to the dark landing. Nurse admitted us with suspicious promptness.

'There you are, Doctor,' she began with relief, but stopped abruptly as she caught sight of John. He followed me into the room and she closed the door behind us. I made a brief introduction, murmuring something vague about a second opinion, and they shook hands, but her eyes turned to mine with a question in them. She was far more jumpy than I was, and she had not even begun to grasp the horror of the situation, poor darling.

I smiled at her as reassuringly as I could and we both watched John, who had walked over to the bed. It was a difficult moment for me. As must have appeared already, my trouble is that I am human.

I followed him slowly, Nurse behind me, every starched yard of her crackling. The bed was a pool of light in the shadowy room. Francia was still completely comatose. Her mouth was open, her flesh dark and terrible. Only her breathing had changed. It was shallower now and very fast. John bent over her, his fingers on her pulse. His eyes were mere slits and his face blank as a wall.

I knew that look. The mantle of impersonal professional interest had dropped over him,

121

shutting out every consideration save one. The woman before him was nothing to him but a faulty machine whose troubles he might be able to cure. I guessed that he had scarcely recognised her. But at the same time I made a bitter discovery about myself. To me she was no interesting machine. To me she was Francia Forde, and while John was present so she would always be.

The routine went on. John scrubbed up and made his examination, with Nurse assisting and growing more and more approving at every stage. I approved myself with what was left of a balanced intelligence. I had never seen him at work before and I understood then why his career had been thought so promising. He had thoroughness and the authority of knowledge, and never for one moment whilst he was at work did a single extraneous thought appear to pass through his mind.

When at last it was over he straightened his back and his face was very grave.

I prepared to make my report to him. Nurse brought the tablets she had found in the sponge bag, and I sent a flush of horror through her cheeks by describing the Dormital in detail. We went into the time factor and Nurse showed her charts. Finally we came to my treatment so far. John kept his eyes on my face, putting in questions and nodding at my answers, and all the time we might have been two other people.

As I finished I saw that he had become haggard. He looked older and even thinner. As I looked at him my own courage began to ebb. The nightmare which was the future settled down over me, more terrible now than it had ever been, since he was in it. Until John had arrived I could have forgiven the woman on the bed. Now, as I looked at her, I found I had not even pity.

'Very sensible and very thorough, Doctor.' He gave me a brief smile as he spoke and it occurred to me that even I was no longer a real person to him either. I tried to achieve some of his detachment.

'Is there anything else?'

'I have used strychnine.'

There was a long silence. I knew that some authorities advocated large doses at comparatively frequent intervals, but the danger was tremendous.

'I thought of it only as a last resort,' I said at last.

He moved his head sharply towards the patient. His voice was very quiet.

'I don't think there's all that time.'

Nurse stood behind him, digesting every word, and I saw her nod to herself vigorously. So it was two to one, and I was overruled. Nurse's opinion carried weight with me. If she saw death it was coming: I had no illusions about that. She had more experience of it than either of us, and there is something about it which does not belong to doctors or books. Its ways are known only to those who have watched for it and seen it steal in again and again through the years.

When John spoke of the size of the dose I felt the sweat break out on my forehead. I had hesitated to give a sixteenth: he was mentioning a sixth. I was on the other side of the bed watching Francia all the time he was talking, and I thought I saw a faint deterioration, an almost imperceptible change. I knew then there was nothing for it. We should have to take the risk.

We made the decision, John and I, with Francia Forde lying senseless between us, and the whole picture was very clear to me. Once we were committed there was a lot to be done, and I found that it was a return to our childhood, and that once again John, with his careful hands and cautious eyes, was the leading spirit and I his faithful assistant. Nurse found it extraordinary. She kept looking at us, her plump face curious but impressed.

Once, when she and I happened to meet at the wash-basin, she ventured to remark on it.

'A grand man. A grand man,' she whispered. 'You'll have known him before, no doubt?'

'All my life,' I murmured back, and let her make what she would of it.

At the last moment there was a hitch. The kettle of freshly boiling water went over in the

124

hearth and Nurse, in a flurry, hurried downstairs for another. John and I were left waiting. It was a trying moment and neither of us spoke. The room seemed to have grown larger and more bare, and I could hear the tick of my wrist watch where it lay on the mantelshelf.

Nurse was a long time and presently I began to walk up and down the rug, aware that my hands were growing wet and that my eyes were sticky. John did not move. He was quite steady. He was looking absently at the expanse of chintz curtains over the windows, his eyes introspective and the muscles of his jaw relaxed and easy. He was worried but not keyed up in any way. I was ashamed of myself.

Nurse returned with a rustle, a steaming kettle in her hand.

'This is a madhouse,' she whispered. 'The servants have gone to their beds and there's no one in the kitchen but a perfect stranger talking to that dratted old cat of a Miss Luffkin of all people.'

I nearly dropped the glass tray I was holding and John, noticing the involuntary movement, drew back the needle in his hand.

'We'll see to all that later. Steady, Ann, please.'

The quiet voice jerked me back to sanity and for the next three minutes nobody spoke at all. In complete silence we tried the last resort, so bold, so dangerous.

I saw the soft flesh of Francia's upper arm pinched between John's fingers. The blue shaft slid deftly under her pale damp skin. Firmly the plunger went home. He dabbed the puncture with the spirit-soaked wool, laid her limp arm gently at her side, and drew the coverlet up to her chin. Then he went to the shelf and glanced at the watch.

'Twenty-five minutes before twelve,' he said, looking at me. 'Nothing to do now but wait . . . and pray.'

I turned down the light by the bed and he went off to the bathroom to wash. Nurse was standing beside me and I leaned towards her.

'Did you say Miss Luffkin was downstairs?'

'Did you ever!' Her eyes were round with indignation. 'Standing there with a milk pudding, every hair of her twiddled into a questionmark. That woman will be snooping in purgatory. The whole town will hear everything, you know. What she saw, and what she didn't. What she thought and what she didn't have time to think. I said to her, "You be off to your bed or that bronchitis of yours will get you and the doctor and I will be too busy to see to you." She soon went. I put the pudding on the side and shut the door after her.'

'And the man?'

'Oh, him? I don't know what he was doing there at all. He wasn't answering her questions, I do remember that. Just stood, holding his pipe politely, as far as I remember. I was busy, you see, getting the kettle to boil.'

'Did he ask you anything?'

It was evident that she had not taken him very seriously. She was so used to running into unexplained people in the houses where she went to nurse.

'I don't think so,' she said at last. 'I remember him saying, "expect you're busy," or something idiotic like that. He was only waiting, that was all.'

'Yes.' My word was hardly as light as a breath. She was right of course. He was only waiting, whoever he was, and I made myself look at the still figure in the bed.

'That woman you were talking about just now.' John had come back without my hearing him. 'Is that the alarming old duck who rushes out with a torch and stops cars?'

'That'll be her, sir.' Nurse spoke with conviction. 'She's lonely. That's the best you can say for her. Did she have the cheek to stop yourself?'

'She did, but I couldn't help her, I fear, and she retired discomfited.'

'So much the better.' Nurse radiated satisfaction. 'She's in the dark, that's what's got under her skin. She's often said to me, 'I'm not inquisitive, Nurse, but I've got to know.''

A faint wry smile touched John's mouth as he met my eyes.

'The vultures gather,' he said softly. 'Nurse,

if there's another room available I should like you to lie down for an hour or two. Dr. Fowler and I will watch the patient, but we ought not to need you until about 4:00 A.M.'

She dared not object. John had made a tremendous impression on her and her instinct was unquestioning obedience. But I could see she didn't like it.

'I'll go down and see what room she can have,' I said quickly, and went out before anyone could demur.

The grandfather clock struck midnight as I crossed the landing and I thought how melodramatic it sounded. It had a very deep chime with an asthmatic wheeze or death rattle between each stroke.

The lights were bright downstairs but the lobby struck chill as I reached it. I crept out of the kitchen. I don't know what I intended to say to the man with the umbrella, if I was anticipating some sort of showdown, or if I just wanted to be sure I had not gone out of my mind and it was really he, but when I pushed open the kitchen door there was no sign of him. Yet the lights were on and it was very warm and bright in there under the heavy beams. The stove was open and a chair by the table had been pushed back as if someone had just risen, but the room was empty.

The back door was closed but not locked and I went on out into a maze of dark pantries and washhouses not wired for electricity. In the middle of an outside passage I fell over a suitcase. It was perfectly ordinary, leather and shabby and fastened with heavy straps. It was just standing there, plumb in the way.

I did not shift it, since it was hardly my affair, and I went back to the kitchen. There a shock awaited me. The chair had been moved. I had left it where I found it, some feet out in the room, but now it was back in its place, its seat neatly under the table. Also, hanging in the warm air, clear and unmistakable, was a blue wisp of tobacco smoke. Yet I had not been more than a few feet out of the kitchen and I had been listening, straining my ears, but I had not heard a sound.

I hurried into the hall and there everything was the same, bare and bright and cold.

Gastineau's voice startled me when I knocked at the living-room door, even though I expected it. He was not in his usual place by the fire, and I glanced round the room nervously. Presently I found him, sitting in a high-backed wing chair which had been pulled up to the desk.

He was tidying a chaotic heap of papers which had covered it, and the wastepaper basket at his side was nearly full. He had moved when I came in and I saw the unspoken question in his eyes. Its eagerness shocked me and I spoke stiffly.

'Miss Forde's condition is unchanged. I came to ask you if I could have a room for

129

Nurse. If she can get a little sleep now it will help.'

'A long day tomorrow, eh? Take any one you like, Doctor. They're all empty.' He spoke brightly. 'The servants sleep at the back, where they have their own staircase, and I shall not go to bed.' He leant back in the chair and pointed to the desk. 'You see? I clean out my pigsty. It is about time and it is as well to do something useful when one is waiting.'

There was the same abominable frankness, the same suggestion that we were allies. I was still recoiling from it when his next remark caught me unaware.

'Dr. Ludlow telephoned but I begged him to excuse my calling you down as you were busy. I took the liberty of telling him that you had brought in Dr. Linnett.' He paused briefly and added, 'He was relieved, and I imagine he has gone to bed. So you see, we are all three here.'

I realised just a little too late that he had checked John's identity very neatly and that this was a gentle reminder that we were all three in it together. Angry with myself and frightened, my only consolation lay in the fact that I saw he was on edge himself. I guessed our combined efficiency was a bit more than he had bargained for. I wished I felt even that much confidence in it.

'Nurse can have any room, you say? Thank you. Good night, Mr. Gastineau. When there is any further news I shall let you know.'

I got out on that and went up again, my knees feeling weak and unreliable.

I found a room with a bed in it which wasn't damp, and I called Nurse out to it. She was very weary but loath to rest while I was still on my feet, but she did as she was told. The sickroom was quiet and airy. John was by the bed as I entered and I went over to him.

'So far so good.'

His narrow eyes were bright in the light of the lamp.

'The lungs are sticking it, that's the mercy. Good vetting of yours, Ann.'

'No reaction yet?'

'No. We'll have to wait. Come and sit down.'

We sat by the fire in the chairs which Nurse and I had pulled up earlier in the evening. John lay back, his dark red head resting against the chintz. His chin was on his breast and I could see the profile that the film people had gone so crazy about when they made the movie which smashed his life and mine. I imagine that we both had the same thought just then. It amounted to a simple question: when, if ever, would he and I be able to sit quietly before a fire and speak freely again? If Francia died, and although I shrank from facing it the chance of her recovery seemed very slender now, the answer was, irrevocably, never. Neither of us would do the cheating, betraying our oaths or laying ourselves open to blackmail. The story was very simple to guess.

There would be a few weeks of agony, gossip and uncertainty, and then . . . what? Who was going to believe the literal truth from either of us? Would I, if I were on the jury?

John turned and caught my eye. The warm light madc his face crimson.

'I fell for the movies,' he said abrubtly.

The intimacy was so very precious to me that I dreaded saying something wrong. Far out of my childhood, a scene at a Christmas party crept into my mind. I saw myself in white silk knickerbockers lashed to a lamp-standard mast.

'The boy stood on the burning deck,' I murmured.

He chuckled. The tears of laughter welled up and stood in his eyes.

'Oh, God, you were funny.'

"Eh-eh, the lassie did her best."

'Father said that, I remember. Oh, you were so angry! You kicked the audience.'

I laughed. 'I made a fool of myself, I know. I still remember that with resentment.'

'Do you?' He was staring back at the fire. 'You didn't make such an ass of yourself as I did Ann, in Italy.'

I took all my courage in my hands.

'It was a bad time just then, just after the war. Victory and nothing else, not even peace.' The words came out lazily, I might have been half asleep.

'That was just about it,' he agreed wearily,

his forehead wrinkling. 'We were just kicking our heels. I was sick of stinks and suffering and useless sacrifices, and these film people were frightfully amusing. I couldn't follow half of what they said, but it all seemed very complimentary. There was one little chap like a sallow Hotei . . . do you remember?'

I nodded. I could see the fat little Chinese god of plenty sitting on Mrs. Linnett's bedroom mantleshelf. John was following my thought.

'I couldn't bear to come back to the empty house, Ann.'

'No. Better not. Hotei was white, by the way.'

'This little guy wasn't. He was grey. I don't know what he was or how he got there, but he was the big noise in the outfit and they were getting special permission to make films outside Florence. I was to be his big discovery, and he went through the Command to get me the necessary leave like a knife going through butter. That's how it happened.'

There was a long silence. I wanted to tell him that it did not matter how it happened, and that I could guess. I wanted to say that I wasn't a fool, and I could imagine what it was like to see a chance of getting away from weary horror, and that I could forgive anybody, let alone him, from shrinking from revisiting that pretty, shabby old house in Southersham where every click of a door latch must have brought him leaping up to meet someone who could never be there again. But I didn't say anything.

Behind us in the dark was the one thing which needed explanation. My throat grew dry and I fidgeted.

'Francia Forde was with them?' I murmured, and held my breath.

'She was about.' His face was hardly so handsome with those deep lines in it.

'You fell for her too?'

'That was a mistake. I knew it. I was a fool.' I felt him draw into himself and the shutters come down between us. 'That's something I can't tell you, or rather, something I won't tell you. Do you mind?'

Mind? Mind? When we had so little time!

'Good heavens, no,' I said. 'I'm dying to talk about myself. I've fallen for whooping cough.'

'Have you?' His interest came back like a light playing over me. 'It's a tremendous subject. Most of the men I see in these days are still prescribing conium and ipecacuanha.'

'Oh, I can do better than that.' I climbed stiffly on my hobbyhorse, while all the time behind us in the gloom lay Francia, hovering between life and death and holding in her limp fingers everything that to us was worth living for. Gradually our talk changed to the diseases of children, and before we knew it our old dreams were out again, hanging like beautiful swathes of coloured material from the cornices.

'I've had my eye on Nurse Tooley for our clinic,' I said.

'What, this one?' He was very interested. 'Yes, she's quite exceptional, isn't she? I noticed that. What's she like with kids?'

'Marvellous.' I started to say it and the word had caught and died in my throat. I bent my head over my hands. There was nothing I could do. The tears ran down my face, over my chin and onto my coat. I stove my body into the chair and struggled with myself, and his hand crept over my elbow and onto my wrist, where it settled like a band of steel.

'Ann . . . oh, Ann.'

It might have been the end of the world.

*　　　*　　　*

I heard it first. My ears, attuned to the faintest nuance in his voice, the slightest sound in the house, picked up the altered breathing from the bed. As I sprang to my feet the other sound came. It was deep, breathy, and quite horribly loud.

We were both on the other side of the room in an instant and John's fingers fumbled as he felt for the lamp switch. Francia lay as we had left her. She was on her back and her hair, like golden seaweed, lay spread across the pillow. But for the first time since I had seen her her eyes were open and as the light reached them

135

they fluttered closed again. Her lips moved and very slowly she turned her head away. My heart turned slowly over in my side, or that was what it felt like. Hardly daring, I put out my hand and took her wrist. The pulse was not so fast. It fluttered no longer.

I looked at John on the other side of the bed. His face startled me. He was radiant. Pure joy looked out of his eyes as he watched her. His lips were half open as if he were helping her, forcing her, to speak.

She woke like the Sleeping Beauty after a thousand years. She was still drugged. Her eyes tried to focus and gave up. Her dry lips moved and she struggled with the clouds which held her. Her will to live was tremendous. I felt it in her pulse. She was fighting manfully. One could only admire her.

I gave her a tiny sip from the cup beside me and she swallowed greedily.

'Francia.' John spoke sharply in the quiet room.

Her great eyes fluttered open and she looked full at him. Recognition was complete. There was even surprise.

'John,' she said in a silly little baby voice, and her small claw of a hand, which still had crimson lacquer on its nails, closed pathetically over his.

In another moment she had gone again. He released himself gently and stood up and wiped his forehead. The dazed, delighted expression was still in his eyes and his voice had a catch in it.

'We've done it,' he said. 'She'll do. That's Phase One. Now, Ann, wake the nurse.'

I could do nothing at all. I turned and went blindly out of the room with a mind which must have been in much the same state as the patient's.

When Nurse came hurrying in, fastening her belt and looking strange and older without her cap, he was walking about the room like a lunatic.

'Broth,' he said abruptly. 'Anything hot and fluid and nourishing. She'll wake up starved in a minute. You did this, Nurse, you and Dr. Fowler.'

'You must take the credit yourself, sir.' She was beaming at him and for the first time I saw little beads on her wide bumpy forehead. So she had been scared too, had she? 'She is so frail, you see, I thought . . .'

'Yes,' he said, looking down, 'so very little.'

I hardly heard him. I went into the bathroom and met a drawn, hard, powerless face with red eyes peering at me out of the mirror. My hair looked as though someone had been trying to pull it off me in a bunch, and my white coat was wet round the neck. My bag was in there and I did what I could with myself, but my hands were shaking and there was something funny about my eyes. They had grown, for one thing, and looked like a tragedy

137

queen's in full make-up.

When I came out, John had fixed himself a high seat where he could command the bed, and he was sitting there, one hand on her pulse, his gaze fixed steadily on her face.

'Damned nearly normal,' he said over his shoulder. 'Do you think I'd raise the house if I burst into song?'

I bit back what I was going to say and made myself very busy.

'I wonder if I ought to go and help Nurse?'

'No. She'll find anything that's there. Nurses like that have six senses. They find sustenance in deserts and under flowerpots. You leave it to her.'

'And the patient to you?'

He didn't even notice my tone. 'Yes,' he said contentedly, 'and the patient to me. Look out.'

Francia stirred again and we gave her water, and I washed her mouth. She was gaining every minute, and every minute I was seeing more and more clearly the sort of person I thought she must be. Her beauty was but the half of it, I suspected.

John cut into my thought 'Of course you don't know her, do you?' he said cheerfully. 'You wait.'

On the last word he bent over her again, and so mercifully did not see my face.

Nurse returned triumphant with a smoking bowl on a tray.

'Just tinned soup,' she apologised, 'but it's a

good kind. Mr. Gastineau had to come out and find this for me himself, or I shouldn't have got a thing. I've told him to send down to the town, wake somebody up and get me some meat extract.'

John waved her to the hearth. He was still in ecstatic mood.

'Keep it hot a minute. She won't be so long now.'

Since there was absolutely nothing for me to do, I sat down in the larger of the two chairs by the fire. My idea was to think out the next step. What were we going to do about Gastineau? The problem of Francia seemed to have been settled. John was attending to that.

The heat crept over me and the relief from the strain of the last thirteen hours was very relaxing. Sleep hit me like a hammer. I felt it and hardly struggled against it. My last conscious thought was that there was nothing, nothing that I could do.

I awoke feeling that I was sailing slowly up an enormous lift shaft, and opened my eyes to see the cold light turning the chintz curtains grey. In the room, very far away, someone was speaking. It was a voice I had never heard before, female and husky and affected, and it said, unless I was still dreaming:

'Not t'irsty, t'ank you.'

I sat up and saw Nurse Tooley looking down at me, a harassed expression on her shining face.

'Well, it's a wonderful thing to be able to sleep,' she remarked. 'I've heard you say so yourself, Doctor. Good morning to you.'

'I say, I'm sorry.' I got up and stretched my cramped legs. John was still at the bedside. I could see his shoulder blades, sharp and weary-looking, showing through the white linen of his coat.

Raised now, on a heap of pillows, her hair combed and her eyes wide open, lay Francia. As I went over I realised that something was different and before I reached the bedside I knew what it was. The entire atmosphere had changed. During all the terror and misery of the night we three had been comrades, linked by a single outlook. Now that was gone. A stranger had arrived.

John got up. He was exhausted and there were dark rings to his eyes.

'Take over, will you? I don't want her to sleep for a bit. See what you think of the general condition.'

'You're going to leave me?' The patient, who was as weak as a fish and still had the drug about her, managed to convey a sort of halfhearted seductiveness and her little hands moved.

'Just for, a while.' John, spoke firmly and kindly and exactly as any other doctor would have done. 'Dr. Fowler will look after you.'

'Vewy well.' Her great eyes rolled away from him and came to rest on me. 'Can you move

140

me? I'm tired. One of my shoulders hurts. I don't know which one. Well, find out, can't you?'

Her speech was still slurred and she must have been only half there, but it was perfectly plain that she had one manner for men and another for women, neither of them guaranteed to have been successful, I should have thought.

In the next twenty-five minutes I learnt about Francia Forde and an hour later I could have written an essay on her, and I was a less jealous but infinitely more puzzled woman. She was the most unsubtle person I had ever met and she had one interest—Francia. She was practically without subterfuge; and greed, which is of all the vices the one most instantly apparent to the average human being, gleamed out of every word and every movement and every look. Her hands were greedy, her eyes were greedy. The moment she was not acting, rapacity appeared. Poor little thing, she didn't even hide it.

Whatever I had expected, it had not been this. Gastineau's story was completely convincing in every particular save the important one. It seemed impossible to me that he should have loved her. Yet, when I remembered that the incident had taken place at the beginning of the war, ten years ago, when she must have been still in her teens, perhaps it was not so difficult. She must have looked like a flower. Perhaps even her greediness had been pretty like a child's.

The thing I did not understand at all was John. He was sitting with his back to me in the chair I had slept in, and I saw his dark head above it. If hc had been taken in, even for an hour, by *this*, he simply wasn't the man I thought he was.

I left Francia to Nurse and went to him. He considered me with narrowed eyes and did not move. His arms were folded and he looked like a sleepy bird.

'What are we going to do with her?' He did not speak aloud but mouthed the words very elaborately, so that I was bound to follow them.

After a bit he tried again. 'Can't leave her here, can we?'

It was the one mood I had not expected. We were in a fine old predicament, the two of us.

'I'll find out.' I spoke with decision. The problem of Gastineau was yet to be solved. Our duty was plain. We ought to remove the woman and inform the police, and yet I shrank from it. I was not a detective . . . or a judge either. Yet one could hardly leave him loose, perhaps to try to kill again. However, I could make him talk. He owed me that at least.

I went out of the room, stepped onto the dark landing, closed the door very softly behind me as a doctor should, and froze.

Seated near the top of the stairs was the

man with the umbrella. He still had it with him, neatly rolled, hanging over the back of the chair. His hat was on his knees.

He rose as I appeared and favoured me with one of his apologetic stares.

'Good morning, Doctor. May I hope that the patient is a little better?'

I was not afraid of him any more. I made the discovery with a stab of delight. Indeed, eying him now, it seemed absurd that I ever had been, he was so meek and gentle-looking.

'Yes, thank you,' I said cheerfully, and was about to pass when he made a most surprising remark.

'I fear everyone else has gone,' he said. 'That was why I thought it best to come up here.'

'Gone?' I repeated stupidly.

'Oh dear.' It seemed to be his favourite expletive. 'I made sure you knew. Otherwise I should have certainly ventured to warn you. But since you had seen Mr. Gastineau destroying his papers I made certain you had guessed his intentions. He and his servants went off in the car soon after the nurse came down for broth. I think she told someone to go for meat extract, but as they all took their suitcases I really don't suppose they will be back.'

It was the longest speech I had ever heard him make. He towered over me and his pale eyes were frighteningly intelligent as they looked down into mine.

'I sincerely hope I've not been unhelpful, but since I heard you trip over the manservant's trunk in the back kitchen I really thought that you were aware that they contemplated flight.'

His excessive formality might have been funny at any other time.

'Where were you?' I demanded.

'I—er—I moved,' he said obliquely. 'I didn't want to introduce myself just then.'

'Who are you?' I nearly said, 'Who on earth on you?' but I had the impression that might have hurt him.

He was very dignified. He produced a card at once, with relief, I thought. Engraved on the pasteboard in fine flowing script were the words:

Reacquaintance Ltd.
Mr. Roland Bluett.

'Oh, a detective agency!' I exclaimed in triumph, and a flush appeared on his high cheekbones.

'We don't call ourselves that, Doctor,' he protested gently. 'We are a very old established firm. We specialise in finding lost people with the maximum amount of discretion. Most of our work concerns lost relatives, of course, but this . . . this was rather different. In this case we represent Messrs. Moonlight, a rather

144

larger concern than our own if not quite so long established.'

'I see,' I agreed slowly.

He sighed. 'I'm so glad,' he said simply. 'I did so fear you might have formed a wrong impression. My clients were merely anxious to make certain that nothing of—er—how shall I say? . . . an unfortunate nature would appear about Miss Forde in the very same newspapers which had arranged to carry their advertisements. You do see, Doctor, that would have been most embarrassing?'

'Do you know how near it might have happened?' I felt unkind as soon as I had spoken. He looked both intelligent and appalled.

'I gathered it,' he said earnestly. 'I've been on tenterhooks, believe me. But my position was particularly difficult since the lady was in the care, and not the very good care, I fear, of her husband.'

My heart jumped violently but I didn't understand him. I stood looking at him blankly until he said primly: 'Miss Forde was married to Mr. Gastineau some years ago in Sweden. We have verified that.' He conveyed that as far as he knew a marriage in Sweden was legal, but not of course so good as it would be in England.

Even in my shaking-kneed condition, I felt that he and Percy should have met.

'Are you sure of this?'

'Oh, without a doubt,' said Mr. Bluett firmly. 'Otherwise my position would have been so much easier, wouldn't it? You would have found me at the front door, Doctor, not the back. It was the return of Mr. Gastineau, virtually from the dead, which has made most of our trouble.'

'But I thought Miss Forde was married to— to someone else,' I said huskily.

He regarded me with horror and said the last thing I had expected.

'Now that really would be intolerable. I know there was an unfortunate publicity story which appeared before she was famous, about some runaway—er—escapade in Italy, but believe me, that was pure fiction. Miss Forde herself assured my clients when they were checking her credentials that there was nothing in it. They understood that she was a widow, Mr. Gastineau's widow. When they learnt that she had vanished after going to dine with her husband, who had so suddenly reappeared, they were naturally anxious, so they put matters in our hands.'

'Because they feared that she might be on the verge of a breakdown?' I murmured cruelly.

He met my eyes very steadily.

'On the verge of a breakdown,' he repeated meekly, and the vague expression crept over his eyes again.

I said nothing. My mind was seething with a

thousand questions and it was some seconds before I heard his polite enquiry.

'When do you think she will be well enough for me to take her back, Doctor?'

When it did sink in I nearly fell over.

'Take her back?' I whispered.

'Naturally.' He was surprised by my stupidity. 'Quite frankly, now that I have found her I have no intention of leaving her side. My clients are in the process of spending two million pounds in publicising their product in advertisements which—er—incorporate her face. Now that Mr. Gastineau has gone, she will hardly want to stay here. I should like to take her back to her flat in London.'

I didn't know what to do. I stood there shaking, wondering whether to tell John at once, wondering whether to clasp dear Mr. Bluett by the hand, wondering whether to sit down and cry with relief. The thing that settled the matter was the most unexpected incident in the whole of that hectic week end.

Downstairs in the front hall somebody coughed loudly and, looking over the banisters, I found myself facing Percy Ludlow and Sergeant Archer. They were both cold and miserable and Percy looked furious. As he saw me he heaved a noisy sigh.

'And Thank God for somebody sensible. Come down, can you? Give this feller some sort of statement.'

Mr. Bluett had faded into the background

like a shadow so I went down to them alone. Percy had his hands in his coat pockets and was stamping on the tiles to keep his feet warm. It was clear that he had been dragged out of bed, for he was unshaven and there was a muffler round his throat.

Archer was in much the same state, except that his uniform hid his lack of collar, and both men were covered with mud. The sergeant was more quiet and paler than I had ever seen him, and it took me some minutes to grasp that this new attitude of his was partly deference and partly shock. Percy surprised me by taking my arm.

'You look tired. Had a bad night? Patient doing?'

'Not bad,' I assured him. 'Sitting up.'

'Eating?'

'A little.'

'That's all right then. Sorry to bring you more trouble, but we can't get on without you. The two survivors can't speak anything but monkey talk.'

'Survivors?'

'Yes.' He blew the word into a bubble. 'Another blessed road smash. And I tell you what, Ann, and I don't mind saying it in front of a policeman, he can take it down if he likes, it's solely the fault of that fool woman.'

'What woman?'

He exploded. 'Why, Lizzie! She was the only woman on the road. Lizzie Luffkin, silly old besom. She admitted to running out to a fast-moving car and shining a torch in the eyes of the driver. I ask you! I hope she gets a reprimand from the court—in fact I'll see she gets it. Car turned clean over. One man died instantly.'

'Who?' I asked, although I think I knew.

Percy patted me. 'Your patient, my dear. Sorry, but there you are. I think I'm right. Osteoarthritis, far advanced.'

'Yes, that's Gastineau.'

'That's all I want to know, Doctor.' Archer was gentle. 'Just the name and approximate age. I can't get a word of sense out of the others.'

Percy stayed with me and when the policeman had gone tried to comfort me, I don't quite know why.

'Poor feller,' he murmured, standing on the doorstep, his legs wide apart, his old eyes roaming the morning scene. 'Poor, poor feller. But still, arthritis. Joints badly affected. He hadn't much to look forward to, had he?'

'No.' I spoke more softly than I had intended. 'No, he hadn't. Nothing at all.'

Nurse and Mr. Bluett stayed with Francia, and before I left Peacocks I rang Mr. Robins again and arranged for the Mapleford ambulance to take her back to London but not to Barton Square. Mr. Bluett, who revealed remarkable resource, fixed for a London nurse to travel with her.

No one appeared to notice that it was a little odd that Gastineau and his servants should have decided to go driving in the dawn with a carful of luggage. Mapleford was so aghast at the accident, and so intrigued by its cause, that it missed the obvious, and the only person who would have been certain to seize on it was not saying very much just then. Poor Miss Luffkin had taken to her bed with the outspoken Wells as her medical attendant.

I took John home to breakfast and Rhoda met us with a look which said as plainly as words that we could tell her what we liked, but as she saw it we'd been out all night. However, since John was so thin she spread herself over breakfast, and while she was cooking and singing 'Careless Hands' with expression, I snatched a bath and he telephoned Grundesberg.

We sat in the sunny window with coffee, homemade bread, and the butter which Rhoda had given her by a woman who knows a cow, and we did not look at each other. The world was quiet and warm and green and I was happy and hungry and curious.

John was happy too. It glowed in him and made him different and exciting and not at all as I had known him as a boy.

After a long time he said abruptly:

'I had a talk with Mr. Bluett, and if he's right about Francia and Gastineau you'll have to have me led around by a keeper, Ann.

Choose someone kind.'

'Is he right?'

'I don't know.' He spoke very slowly, putting out his hand to find mine. 'The thing that makes it credible is the otherwise unbelievable attitude of Messrs. Moonlight and Company.'

'Why?'

'Well, my dear girl, a concern of that size doesn't merely choose a pretty face, however famous. It's a serious business, that sort of advertising. They must have examined her record very carefully before they risked using her in a scheme as vast as that. If she said she was Gastineau's widow they'd have spotted any legal second marriage, or so I should have thought.'

I turned round to him, put my hands on his shoulders and looked into his face.

'It's time I had that story, John.'

His face was close to mine, but there was no deeper colour in it and his eyes were thoughtful rather than ashamed.

'Now we've saved her silly little life for her, I don't seem anywhere near so sore,' he observed unexpectedly. 'That was why I was so thrilled when I saw her reviving, I suppose. My God, she made a monkey out of me.'

'What was this?' I burst out with some asperity. 'A shotgun wedding?'

That annoyed him and his arms closed round me to make certain of me while he talked. In some ways he had not changed since he was ten.

'I didn't write and tell you about the film offer because I knew that you'd never approve of my giving up medicine, and I wanted to get it all fixed before you could advise against it,' he announced with all the peculiar irritability of a man making a confession.

'Very wise,' I murmured.

He sighed and pushed my head down on his shoulder.

'I told you. I fell for the movie offer and I helped push the thing through with the army. The company was going to make a film with the old French stage star, Mme. Duse, a wonderful old dear, Ann. She had a face like a duck but she could make you laugh or cry at will. I was to be the young army officer, bursting with charm and verisimilitude, who was to make hay with her daughter's heart as I came charging in with my men to liberate 'em all.'

'Yes, I see all that.'

'I don't think you do,' he said grimly. 'I was so dead keen and so were all my buddies in the regiment. Some of 'em were to be loaned for small parts, and we were like kids about it all. The war was over and this was the first pleasant thing to happen to us for years. Unfortunately, I was teacher's pet and I didn't know the ropes at all. There's a hell of a lot of jealousy in that business, Ann.'

'I believe you,' I laughed and he pushed my

head down again.

'It's not quite as you think, all the same. The movies are a much more chancy business than most, and publicity seems to mean such a hell of a lot to everybody. You see, until the little director chap discovered me, and got a story with me about my being given indefinite leave because I was just what they wanted and typical and all that, until then the *daughter* was supposed to be the second most important person in the show.'

'Oh, I see. And she was to be played by Francia?'

'Exactly. Francia had been spotted playing "bits" in Sweden and had been sent over for the part. She was a go-getter in her way. At least she wouldn't let anything stand in it. But unfortunately when she arrived I had appeared on the scene, and seemed all set to steal her thunder.'

He paused. 'Mind you, there was not a great deal of thunder to go round. We only had what Mme. Duse left. However, the director had become sold on me and he had the script writers enlarge my part. The result was that it didn't look as if Francia's big chance was going to get her very far.'

'Did she make it clear that she resented that?'

He grinned. 'Not to me. I suppose I was the only soul in the outfit who had no notion what was happening. My idea was to act. I didn't

153

know there was any more to the job. God, I was green! Francia began by snubbing me, and then, after she'd had a good look round, suddenly made a dead set at me. I wasn't attracted and I kept out of her way. That's why what happened took me completely by surprise.'

He hesitated. 'I think I exasperated her,' he said at last. 'Anyway, just as all the preliminary publicity was going out she gave a party. I couldn't get out of going. I drank what I was handed and after that it was the Bristol Splice trick pure and simple.'

I wriggled my head round to look at him and sat up.

'What's that?'

He was sneering, his fastidious nose contemptuous.

'The Bristol Splice is the trick that in the seventeenth century the ladies of the town used to play on those prudent sailors who had left their pay with the mate, my dear. I didn't remember the end of the party, and when I did wake, with my head on fire, it was the day after tomorrow so to speak. I was in a country hotel bedroom, Francia was dancing about in a negligee, and a friend of hers—one of the lads who wrote publicity—was showing a pack of Italians, whom he said were newspapermen, a picture of Francia in a wedding dress and an Italian civil marriage certificate. Everybody was drinking our health.'

'What did you do?'

He smiled angrily. 'Oh, same like the sailors, I'm afraid. It's a time-honoured reaction, except that I had the presence of mind not to talk. I knocked out the publicity writer and, while Francia was reviving him, dressed hurriedly in the bathroom and lit out of the window. So ended my movie career.'

'But, darling,' I protested, 'didn't you go back to the film people at all?'

He shrugged his shoulders. 'Where was the use? I'd got it into my head that the certificate was genuine. I made certain I was trapped. If I made a row I damned myself and the film, and if I didn't, well, I had Francia on my hands. Besides . . .'

'Besides what?'

He gave me a curiously timid glance from under his lids.

'I thought I was probably better medicine. Oh, have a heart, Ann! I'd come smartly out of the rose-pink fog. I was sick to death of the whole lot of 'em.'

I sat thinking. He might at least have told me. And yet I knew a little of the odd mental conditions which appeared in men who had suddenly been released from years of active service. For a time some of them had developed the self-consciousness which would have been considered excessive in a Victorian miss of seventeen.

We were still holding hands and I moved a

little nearer to him.

'You'd better find out about the marriage now.'

'Good lord, yes.'

I couldn't resist it. 'Lucky I waited,' I observed.

He pulled me close to him and kissed me squarely on the mouth.·

'I had my eye on you all the time.'

'What?'

'I found out where you were when I got back. Then I had to get a job and I had to make good at it. Last week I thought the time had come and I set about breaking things to you gently. I began by letting it be known in Southersham that the prodigal had returned. I knew someone would pass it on.'

I sat up at that.

'Do you mean to say that you were conceited enough to expect me to approach you?'

He pulled me back again and chuckled.

'Hang it,' he said, 'I got a telegram.'

Rhoda stopped the fight by appearing in the doorway, the morning papers in her hand.

'See here.' Her voice was packed with admiration. 'Look at that Miss Francia doing her washing. Doesn't she look lovely? All over a whole page!'